THE LISTENER

BO HUSTON

THE LISTENER

A Novella and Four Stories

ST. MARTIN'S PRESS
New York

Design by Sara Stemen

Library of Congress Cataloging-in-Publication Data

Huston, Bo
    The Listener : a novella and four stories / Bo Huston.
        p.   cm.
    ISBN 0-312-09931-2 (hardcover)
    I. Mothers and sons—California—Fiction. 2. Gay men—
California—Fiction.   I. Title.
    PS3558.U7797L57   1993
    813'.54—dc20   93-11463
                                                            CIP

First Edition: October 1993

10 9 8 7 6 5 4 3 2 1

—for my parents

CONTENTS

THE LISTENER

Like the sound of the flute, heard far away on the banks of some river in the hour of dawn, and regarded as but one amongst many sweet songs of the world; and like the same strain when the listener has drawn nearer and nearer and at last with his whole mind on the music, has become himself the player . . .

—SISTER NIVEDITA, 1910

PART I

I

The windows of Jane's kitchen were open wide, for it was a dreary and still summer evening. Moths circled and threw themselves recklessly against the torn screen door. The porch was lit by a yellow bulb which cast a wide cone of light onto the black-and-white checked floor by Jane's feet, and with the crazy bouncing shadows of those moths it seemed like firelight.

"I'm just to the point where I don't really like anyone anymore," Jane said, in a resigned tone. She gently tapped a boiled egg with a spoon, cracked the shell thoroughly and peeled it off, dunked the white rubbery egg in water, then placed it in a bowl with the others. "I used to like my sisters. Liked them enough, anyway. But then it seemed they didn't really understand me. They were mean to me.

"And men. I knew about men a long time ago. What there is to like about them, and what there is *not* to like." Jane gave a short, joyless laugh, and her shoulders lifted, then fell. "But, we won't go into all that," said Jane. "You're too young for all that." She twisted her head to look around; she smiled. "What's that you've got?"

"Earring," said Russell.

"Well, look at you."

Russell shook his head and the cheap piece of jewelry, made of gold-colored tin and bits of shiny green glass, swung from his right ear.

"Well, that's very fancy," Jane said, and turned back to her work. She chopped the egg fine and cut an onion, then mixed them in a wooden bowl and added some mayonnaise, some pepper, and salt. Meanwhile, macaroni had been cooking on the stove; she drained it over the sink and stirred everything together. "My special egg-and-noodle salad," she said, stepping back and regarding the concoction. Then: "Russell, wipe off that table now, and put down some plates and forks."

"Plates and forks. Plates and forks," the little boy echoed as he did his chore.

And when they were seated across from each other, it was nearly dark outside. Crickets clicked and purred somewhere behind the house. From the neighbor's place up the road could be heard piano music, and the sound of a glass breaking and a woman's squeaky laughter.

Jane took a bite of her salad, then tapped her chin with her fork. "You know, there are two types of people in the world. Some are the social types. That's just their temperament—to be involved, to know everyone. They're always laughing, running off to some party or playing some game. You'll see them all through your life, Russell," she said seriously, but she was not looking at the boy. "Then, there are other people who are just the lonely kind. Stay to themselves. They're thinking all the time, they're quiet. They don't want anything to do with anyone else. Those are the two kinds of people, Russell. You watch, and you'll notice it." She tapped her fork on the table.

"What kind are you, Jane?"

Jane laughed heartily now, revealing her discolored, uneven teeth. She put a dirty hand flat on the top of her head. "Well, let's see. Well—I'm both. I mean, I've *been* both."

Russell lowered his head and, as though they were telling scary secrets, he whispered: "What kind am *I?*"

"You? Well, we'll have to see. We'll just have to wait and see."

After their supper, Jane pushed back her chair, sat with her legs apart and her feet braced on the rungs. She stretched her arms straight above her head, opened her mouth wide in a silent yawn.

"Read to me?" Russell asked softly.

His father must have been an Indian, Jane was thinking, for the boy's hair was so black and straight, it shone; and his skin, especially in this evening light, was a copper color. Jane had not known the father. She only dimly remembered the night, nearly six years ago—sweltering, long, sad. Jane sitting at a corner table of the old Martin's Tavern, hoping some man would speak to her and offer her a drink. One very old man did wink at her; he sat beside her and felt her bare leg.

"What is your name?" she'd asked him.

"Terence."

"Terence, do you want to go with me?"

The old man said nothing.

"Terence," Jane said, more intently, "I'll go to your house. Or in your car."

Terence's expression was puzzled, then embarrassed; but at least he was not laughing at her.

"I'm not kidding," Jane demanded, without blinking. "Even just behind the tavern, back near where those crates are piled up. I'll do whatever you want."

Terence nodded and rose and moved toward the bar. Jane pushed a stray bit of hair behind her ear, sat up straighter as she waited for Terence. But then he was gone.

Then there was another man, a man who worked at the phone company, and all she could remember of him was that his eyebrows were too thick, that they joined in the middle, over the bridge of his nose, and that she could not stop staring. Jane remembered that he might have offered her a ride, or a drink, or money, and that she had told him he looked like a monkey, and he was insulted.

By the time she met the man she believed to be Russell's father she was very drunk—her temples were pounding, she felt nauseated. He had a room above the tavern. She recalled a brown, muscular shoulder, white teeth, a thick neck. Also, some kind of scab just behind his ear. He caressed her hips with big hands, but Jane was impatient and pulled his belt open, tugged at his trousers. The man laughed and called her a cruel name, and Jane, trying to sit on his bed, fell hard to the floor. He was above her. She reached out and took hold of his penis angrily, urgently, as though it were the rope to a church bell and it was Jane's job to sound an alarm.

That was Russell's father, she was fairly certain. And looking at little Russell now, he must have had Indian blood. Jane reached across the table and gently pushed a stubborn curl of her son's hair from his forehead. "Have to get your hair cut soon, Russell. When school comes, I want you to look nice. People have enough to say about me in this town. I'm not going to have them saying I don't know how to keep my boy's hair cut nicely."

Russell shook his head, so the earring swung wildly, and then it came undone and clattered to the floor and rolled under his mother's chair. "Read to me?" he asked again.

2

Dear Meg,

A quick note . . . I'm dashing around like mad (but you say I always am). Great news about Audrey—that she's saying so many new words. My calculations have her at seventeen months old, since she was about six and a half months when I last saw her. She didn't know words back then, but she giggled a lot. Has her hair stayed that funny carrot-red? When will you bring her out to visit me?

Anyway, I really am flying too fast to write a long, nice letter. I'm sorry to hear things are so rough for you there. Cramped apartment, sweltering summer. You've always hated Manhattan anyway; how long is your job going to keep you trapped there? Or is it at Bert's insistence? I cringe and bristle, imagining you schlepping on a subway with a kid under one arm and a bag of groceries under the other, that husband of absolutely no help and criticizing you on top of it all. You're brave and beautiful in your struggles, Meg. You always have been that way. You deserve some easy times. . . .

Anyway—I've been offered a sort of vacation. Remember I told you George had moved from the city to a little town up the coast? Well, he bought a house there—he calls it a cabin—and it is only a couple of hours away. It is right on the ocean, not too near other homes. So, George has to go back east, Boston, for a month, to lead a photography workshop at the university. He offered me his place and, Meg, I did not hesitate for one second. Right—I, who everyone thinks am too afraid to leave San Francisco, or too lazy or too snotty or too crazy. The jokes are always about my dependence on urban life—"How would he possibly manage without the telephone, radio, television, tape player? Without traffic and lights and bars and stores? Without sex?"

And I'm not denying any of that. But off I go to remoteness, deprivation. A primitive, rough month ahead of me.

I don't even know why I'm so eager to go. Adventure, partly. I've been very content these days, Meg, and so I feel expansive, brave. Who needs a dishwasher anyway? Who needs the daily paper? Who needs a telephone answering machine? The idea of casting aside all the devices, gadgets, and information I use to get through each day seems liberating. Classes don't begin again for six weeks. I've thrown a few shirts, a sweater, a couple of pair of pants in a bag (and a carton of cigarettes). I'm ready to go.

Don't laugh at me, Meg. Don't be cynical. I've packed my cameras, too, of course.

I'll shoot some pictures. That is really at the heart of this impulsive trip—I'm so tired of talking about photography, of leading seminars and workshops and lecturing on Diane Arbus or Robert Frank or Helen Levitt or whoever. I need to take some pictures. In my grown-up life I'm a teacher, an expert, and it can start to seem that what I do is think. *So I forget that, really, what I do is* see. *I sometimes lose that sense of myself as visual, as feeling myself and understanding the world through taking pictures—the release of the shutter articulates more for me than publishing articles or lecturing in classrooms. It's me . . . it's been me as long as I can remember. You actually put it best—when I was about eleven and I was always carrying around that beat-up old Nikon of Dad's, you said: "Paul was born with a camera instead of a right eye."*

So I'll take some pictures and go for long walks. I'll chop wood for the stove. And sex? In this town up the California coast, I'm certain there are no handsome, inebriated young men just waiting to be shoved into taxis and taken home. Will I make it through a month of abstinence? (I can see you shaking your head no as you read this.)

For August your little brother is a rugged loner, one with nature. Thoreau. But happier than Thoreau, I think. I'll write you when I get there.

All my love,
Paul

P.S. I forgot to say that I'm expected to take care of George's dog, a cranky thing named Cindy. Only another inconsistency—me with a dog. Wish me luck!

3

Dear Meg,
I am here. I left the city early this morning, driving that old orange Volkswagen bug—I hardly ever use it anymore. A gorgeous ride, if a bit treacherous. California is crazy, wild country, particularly along the coast road. But green and fresh, exhilarating. I pulled over several times to take pictures.

Anyway, the address is on the envelope—a post-office box—so please write. The house is charming, very sturdy, made all of a reddish wood, with large windows. Really, the place is one enormous room—kitchen against the back wall; a handsome antique desk to the right; bed to the left; a couple of armchairs and a table in the center. An unheated bathroom is behind the kitchen. The ceiling is peaked, with beam supports. The furniture is simple, but attractive, and there are lots of books. There is electricity: plugs in the kitchen area and extension cords tacked along the floorboards to every other part of the house. No television or radio, though, and no phone. There are oil lamps and candles for light.

I got here about noon, dropped my bag by the door, and was faced with seven pages of instructions George had left for me—mostly regarding Cindy. She takes special eye drops and ear drops and vitamins and has three different kinds of dog treats; she also has a skin disease that requires ointment; her food must be measured, she has to be fed at specific times, and I'm expected to watch her while she eats; when she's outside I'm supposed to make sure she doesn't chew on certain kinds of weeds (George actually drew little sketches of them!); and, of course, her nails have to be cleaned, with a toothbrush. As I studied the pages, Cindy watched me warily through her beady, diseased eyes. "Maybe you should just be put out of your misery," I said to her, and she growled. Actually bared her teeth.

So I gave Cindy her meal and watched her; she growls even as she chews. I guess she's just not used to me yet.

Later—

I've met a strange person here. His name is Ancer Peak. How's that for a name?

It keeps raining, so I've been stuck inside; it has been pleasant enough, though, reading, feeding the fire in the stove, listening to the torrents on the roof and skylights: like millions of sharp needles. Cindy, when she is ready to go outside, simply walks to the door and barks once—hoarsely, more a grunt, really—then glares at me. When she's ready to be let in, I hear that same arrogant bark; I open the door and she enters, shakes wetness onto my trousers, and walks back to her disgusting chewed and stained pillow on the floor by the stove.

In the late afternoon, since the rain had let up, I decided I should go down to the store and lay in some provisions for supper and tomorrow's breakfast. The store is called Moxie's and looks like the set from some 1930s movie. It is a grainy, black-and-white place. Tall wooden shelves are dusty, sagging under boxes and cans. Noisy, ancient refrigerator cases keep the perishable goods and beer. Every inch of the walls and floor is put to some use: rakes and brooms and shovels are hanging, lightbulbs and baskets are stacked in corners, racks display greeting cards and magazines, and signs for soda pop and cigarettes are placed unevenly around the door. It is dark in Moxie's, too cluttered and old.

When I entered, the door's tin bell clinked. Two women, leaning on their elbows at the counter, were deep in discussion. They went rigid and silent immediately. I smiled at them. "It's really pouring out there," I said, and they nodded at me, barely perceptibly, in unison, and said nothing. I went through the few aisles, picking out some cans of soup, a loaf of bread, milk, butter, coffee. I brought it all to the counter and felt, really, like someone on trial—no, like someone who looked exactly like one of their dead relatives and they just couldn't believe it, they were speechless and afraid of this ghost. The one at the cash register rang up my purchases, and the other one put everything in a paper bag.

"Hello?" came from behind me, along with the door's clinking bell. "Is that Paul?"

I turned to see a squat little man. His chest was deformed in some way—no, not really deformed, just too big for the rest of his body. He had orange hair and a broad grin. He walked toward me, extending his hand. "I'm Ancer Peak. You must be Paul. George told me you'd be coming up this week." We shook hands. "Hello, ladies," he addressed the women. I knew instantly this man was gay, but couldn't say how I knew. The voice, bearing. He was not at all a sexual being; really the opposite. It's a spooky intuition with us gay people, mutated into our sensibility for protection and alliance. We just know.

Not that it mattered much that this little fellow was a homosexual. "Your name again?" I asked.

"Ancer Peak."

I heard the words, but they did not make sense to me, they did not sound like they could possibly be someone's name, and so I looked puzzled.

"Ancer," he offered. "Like Dancer without the 'd'. And Peak. Like Greek. Ancer Peak." He said this little rhyme as though he'd said it many times before.

"I see. Well, it's nice to meet you. And you're a friend of George's?"

"Oh, known him many years. In fact, I'm the one convinced him to come up here and look for a place. You and Cindy getting along fine?"

"So far, so good," I answered. "It'll take some time."

"I was taking care of her before you came. Those drops. But she's a sweet thing," he said, and smiled warmly. (But is she sweet? She has not been sweet to me.) "And everything at the house all right? It's very primitive there. Maybe you'll want to have a phone installed?"

"Well, I thought about it but, actually, I'm looking forward to living . . . simply. Kind of an experiment."

Ancer Peak, a foot or so shorter than I, looked up at me, smiling, but seeming not to comprehend. His eyes were a little bit crossed. After a moment, he said: "Well, if there's anything you want, anything at all, I live just down the road from this store, just to the left there," and he pointed. "And please let me have you over for supper some evening."

"That would be very nice, I'd like that," I said. You know, just as the appropriate response to an invitation.

But Ancer Peak suddenly frowned. "Unless, of course, that would fuck up your experiment." He'd said it quickly, with a low monotone. A mean, abrupt attitude, strikingly different than even a few seconds before.

I was stunned. I almost laughed, but he did not seem to be joking.

Then, the generous smile returned. "Yes, and I have a piano. Do you play? Well, let me get my ice cream and race home before it starts raining hard again. I love ice cream."

I am supposed to phone George tomorrow at three o'clock California time, from the pay phone at the hotel in town. I'll ask him about this creepy Ancer Peak character. Also, on my walk back from Moxie's, I saw a woman, all in black, with a beret, dragging a little boy by the hand; she took huge, angry strides and the little boy was sort of skipping to keep up with her. Woman and boy each carried roller skates, swinging them by the laces. They turned down a path and walked up onto the porch of a huge, rickety old place. So, I want to ask George about this strange pair, and any other eccentric neighbors I should know about.

Love,
Paul

P.S. Why I've embarked on this month of solitude. Maybe you guessed: it's Mark, too. Three months since Mark died. For a year or so before that I had been traveling back and forth from San Francisco to L.A., meeting with his nurses (whom he insulted continually), driving him around, trying to feed him mashed potatoes and ice cream to add weight. I'd sit in a chair by his bed, not even sure he knew I was there. The little house was boiling hot, all the heaters turned on and the windows closed. And Mark had to have the T.V. always blaring—game shows and talk shows and shopping shows. At the end, Mark was on morphine pills that made his lips tremble and his fingers grasp at the edge of his blanket while he slept. I used to watch these involuntary movements, like I was watching a little baby in a crib: delicate, sweet motion for no other purpose than to feel, to reach.

Immediately after his funeral, there was a conference I had to attend, then school started, then I had a grant proposal to write. I drove along hazy, endless Sunset

Boulevard, past electronics stores and doughnut shops and realtors and dentists and health-food stores, out of that town, away. And then, a few hours later, I was on a desolate stretch of Highway 5, heading north. There are miles and miles of windmills, set on top of and between dry, perfectly shaped tan mounds of earth; hundreds of these aluminum machines, light as the air they stir, but powerful. I pulled the car over and stood on the hood to take photographs of this landscape. I thought it was so beautiful and sad and strange. I thought that this extraordinary sight might be able to illuminate something about Mark, and his death, and death and life and me. The pictures did not come out at all well. The pictures do not reveal the awe I felt.

So, it's that ever since he died, I've had the uneasy feeling that grief did not happen—it's waiting for me. Maybe not even tears or a rush of excruciating memories; but some sight or sound that will inform me that this cranky old friend of mine is really gone, that I will not see him again.

So many friends have died from AIDS now. I'm not even troubled anymore by a lot of guilt feelings or romantic speculations. A few years ago, I'd go to memorial services of people who'd died of AIDS, and the tragedy, the waste was shocking, seemed unbearable. Now, services have come to be routine gestures; a few of us hang out on the church steps, smoking cigarettes, distinctly unhysterical. People crack a few jokes. We've all got so used to this horror.

So now I say: thank God I am free of Mark, of the trauma of his illness, of agonizing along with him—and I don't even think I'm a monster for feeling free.

The day I phoned Mother and told her Mark had died, she was very kind and said: "Well, Paul, isn't he really better off, though?" Because he was nothing but knees and elbows, because he could not even hold his head up, because he had to wear diapers to bed and be fed through a tube, because his crazy eyes were not crazy anymore, just vacant . . . because the man was wasting to nothing, well, yes, you can say he's now better off. What I said to Mother, though, was: "You know, I'm getting really tired of concluding that all my friends are better off dead." Silence. I really did know what she meant, and that her intention was to comfort. I did not mean to hurt her feelings. But I think she doesn't . . . understand.

Now it was only Jane and the little boy living there. In the last house, where the road curved, under a mean tangle of electrical wires, almost to the edge of the cliff, near the sea, but in a shadow. Once there had been a whole family: Jane's mother and the sisters. The girls all were pretty, with long, reddish hair. The mother had that hair. Hadn't the mother been ill?

It was a silent, dull town. The bandstand in the center square, no longer used, was weathered and covered with wild vines. The post office, the diner, and the bank were singularly uninviting, poorly kept up, only functional. Once, soldiers had come here at night to get drunk; and their voices and loud music could be heard from Martin's Tavern. But the army base was long closed down; its unpainted buildings stood dead behind tall metal fences. Martin's was gone now, too, the wooden building turned into a realty office. Nice towns, closer to the city, with fancy seafood places and good hotels, claimed the tourists. No one ever came here.

The men of the town worked at a lumber mill some twenty miles north, and drank in highway bars on their way home. Women took care of the town, and of the families and homes. People in this town, when they were shocked, made their lips tight and thin, they blinked slowly, then seemed to look away. Opinions were uttered around oilcloth-covered kitchen tables, between sips of warm black coffee, shared in low tones on porches or over fences or in an aisle at Moxie's market. People were frequently shocked about Jane.

"She's dirty," said one neighbor, Constance Welch. "That's my problem with her, right there. If she'd clean up that old stringy, raggedy hair, if she'd put on something nice once in a while instead of that old baggy old dress she wears . . ."

"Or how about those trousers she walks around in?" agreed Constance's divorced daughter, Fern. "And those big old brown boots . . ."

"Just look how she keeps that house," Shirley observed. "Walter went in there to fix her icebox—last summer? after that storm? everyone's electricity went crazy?—and he said he'd never seen anything like it. Never seen anything like it. Stuff all over the place. Clothes. Books and papers. Bags and boxes full of junk in the corners. And practically pitch-black darkness in that house. She keeps all the shutters done, the lights out."

"She's always trying to save on the electric bill," Constance whispered, as though this were a scandalous fact.

"I know that. Had the nerve to wrangle with Walter over what he charged her. I told Walter, I said: 'You might as well just have let her food all go rotten.' And you know what Walter told me?"

From Fern and her mother in unison: "What?"

"Said there was hardly any food even in that old refrigerator."

"Oh, she's just cheap. 'Stead of curtains, she hangs up those dirty old pillowcases."

"Disgrace. Sad for the little boy, though."

One day at Moxie's, old Joseph told his friend Sam: "I knew her mother very well. Beautiful woman, very pleasant, good-tempered. And Jane was a sweet thing when she was a girl. Polite. Just a sweet thing. All those sisters were sweet." And Sam said: "Oh, no. That's not what I heard at all. Not at all. And wasn't the mother ill?"

Jane was slightly over six feet tall. Her hair was dark and hung limply to below her shoulders. She did not wear makeup; she spent little time outdoors, so her face was white and plain. Her every appearance was a small event, worth remarking upon—as she walked along the wide main street of the town, keeping her head straight; or when she drove past in her huge, rusting tan Pontiac. Even to see her standing on her porch, as she often did, holding a mug of coffee, smoking a cigarette, gazing off at the cloudless, starless black sky. Carrie from the diner, Truman from the realty office, Cleary the locksmith—these people had all gone to school with Jane, had seen her all their lives.

Ancer Peak, her neighbor, had had some terrible arguments with Jane about his piano playing and his parties. Jane called them "parties"; Ancer Peak said he just liked to have a few friends over for drinks.

Mrs. Listerbrook had been principal at the school years ago; she'd retired and had won prizes for the rosebushes in front of her house on High Street, and the State of California had designated that house a historic landmark. Mrs. Listerbrook remembered Jane as a teenager and always had felt sorry for her. "Jane never fit in somehow. Some people are just different, they don't fit in."

Of course, it was one thing to observe Jane, to comment, to snicker, to think she was comical, sinister, strange—some kind of monster. Russell, though, her little boy, was the sad part of the story.

But Jane did not worry about the town. She did not care a bit what gossips said or thought. She'd seen and heard them all her life. She certainly did not worry about the world—politics and war and government. There was a time when Jane subscribed to the local newspaper, *The Ledger,* because she was interested in news of the space flights; but as the astronauts and their missions were reported about less and less over the years, Jane saw no reason for a daily paper. She canceled her subscription—sending a brief note to the editor, Mr. Singer, expressing her dissatisfaction with his publication's lack of interest in the scientific advances being made by NASA. Singer wrote back to Jane—sorry she no longer wished to subscribe, but would she please pay her outstanding bill? No one could remember Jane's rationale for refusing to pay, and she and Singer fought for months. The editor's strategy was to simply continue to deliver the morning *Ledger* to Jane's porch, and Jane would leave it there, folded, untouched; and a pyramid of newspapers formed beside her front door. Eventually, she approached a lawyer in town, a Mr. Barrie, with the idea of suing Singer and his paper for littering on her property. Barrie spoke calmly to Singer, both men shaking their heads, for all this nuisance was hardly worth either of them wasting their time. Poor Jane, just crazy and stubborn.

"Always has to get her own way," was Fern's opinion.

"The sisters were like that too, you ask me," Constance thought.

Jane did not concern herself about good music, or having a fun time, or what was playing at the movies. She did not like the Fourth of July parade or the town meetings. She did not give any thought to other people—she'd learned not to. And she had no thoughts of love, either. Love had been very much on Jane's mind when she was a girl, but now she did not think of it.

What Jane did worry about was money. After supper, the fog eased toward the cliffs and settled over their house; the air was cool, the sky purple-gray. Jane cleared the table, arranged her pads of paper, notebooks, and file folders in neat piles. She sat before this business wearing half-glasses, her hair tucked behind her ears, rolling the end of a pencil between her teeth.

"Storm coming," her little boy said, kneeling on a chair by the screen door, looking out.

"Don't bother me now, Russell. I have to do my figuring. Why don't you go around and light the lamps, it'll be dark soon." This project Russell did conscientiously and expertly, holding a box of wooden kitchen matches in his hands, carefully lifting the glass globe of each lamp, striking a match, touching the flame to the wet wick, replacing the globe. And the boy wore a small, delighted, private smile as the lamp suddenly cast its glow.

"See, that's a way we save electricity," Jane said, satisfied. She flipped to a page in one of her notebooks and dated it at the top. Then she drew lines down the page to form columns. She had devised her own system for categorizing and assessing the financial accounts; it was something only she could comprehend; and it was not subject to change, really. Jane despised spending any money at all. Those normal expenditures of one's life, as for food, clothing, household items, gas for the car, Jane resented as though she had been robbed. At Moxie's, when she purchased a pack of cigarettes and some bread, her conception of the transaction was that she had taken what she needed and been forced to give away her cash.

In the half an hour during which Jane checked and rechecked her financial affairs, darkness would come. Little Russell would be curled into the stuffed armchair with some volume of the *Encyclopaedia Britannica,* 1959 edition. Jane had told him that if he had looked at every page in the encyclopedia, by the time he got to school he'd be far ahead of the other kids. Sleepily, with "LO to MED" on his lap, he would struggle to turn the pages, to look at the photographs and ink drawings and maps, to follow the lines of words with his finger—unfathomable but familiar squiggles and dots. Sung to sleep by the tuneless lullaby of his mother's pencil scratching and an owl's uneven hooting, and the wind.

Jane pulled off her glasses, furious. She needed new locks on her front door and windows and Cleary, that thief, had given her an outrageous estimate, told her some lies about having to send away for materials. "Can't trust anyone," Jane whispered. "Can't count on anyone to be fair, to give a person a break."

She rose and went to her sleeping son. She thought of picking him up, of carrying him to bed; but she could not make herself lean over and touch him. "Russell," she said. "Russell. Up to bed now."

The boy blinked and smiled, rubbed an eye with his knuckle.

"Up to bed now, Russell."

"Up to bed, okay, Jane. You go to bed too now?"

"In a while. Come on."

Jane preceded her son up the short staircase, carrying a lighted lamp before them. His room was at one end of the second-floor hallway; the window overlooked the road. She jerked her chin at his bed. "Hop in," she instructed the boy, and he did. He nestled under two quite worn quilts, and Jane asked if he was too cold, if he wanted another blanket. He shook his head, smiling.

"On your back now, Russell. Flat on your back, you know how," said Jane, softly, but with some impatience. The little boy complied. "Are you all ready?" Russell nodded.

Jane reached under the bed and pulled out a length of sturdy brown rope; it was attached by a nail to the bed frame, and Jane walked around the bed and looped it through a hook on the opposite side, so that the rope was stretched across her son's chest. Three more such restraints were used: one across his middle, one for his knees, one for his ankles. With Russell secured into his bed, Jane curled two fingers under the ropes, to see that it was firm but not too tight, and then she asked: "Can you breathe okay?"

"Yes. I can breathe."

And Jane gave one last look, up and down her son's bound figure. Satisfied, she gave a short nod and left his room, saying: "Good night now, Russell. Shut your eyes, because I'm about to take out the light." She closed the door gently. Suddenly his small, square, warm room was a long gray-and-black shadow. An empty room, now. Russell shut his eyes tight, so he would not see the shadowed room, or know its emptiness.

5

Dear Meg:
2 A.M.—
It's my first night. The storm lasted through the evening. The rain seems to have let up, but there is still a strong wind. I can hear the sea, even feel it—a mighty thud against the cliffs shakes the floorboards. The sea is discontented, I think. Because it is big, but not big enough; powerful, but not powerful enough. And so it pounds the land resentfully. Maybe the sea is mad at me.

I am in the center of this enormous, strange bed, wearing one of George's old sweatshirts, covered by two colorful, ragged quilts. The fire is dying in the wood stove. An oil lamp casts a shimmering, scented glow across the rough wood walls. Among the more scholarly and classic literature on George's shelves, there is plenty of trash: old British Gothic novels, detective stories, movie-star biographies. Wonder where he hides his pornography.

Right by George's bed is a beautifully framed photograph of Ken. I think you met Ken once. As I recall, you liked Ken but were not very fond of George. Did you know they were together for a decade? A couple of years ago, Ken had an affair with some young kid, a heroin addict. Scandal! There followed a year of gruesome stories, long stretches of emptiness, waiting, crises. George would call me, too dazed and frozen to cry.

George and I were friends from college—he was one of the more beloved photography teachers and I was his assistant. Over the years, we've seen each other through three or four demented boyfriends. I did not even know Ken very well. I heard about him a lot, though—usually terrible stories of lies and cheating, fights. He was younger than George, and a flirt. I was biased of course in George's favor, always felt animosity toward Ken. I used to urge George to dump him. George never did, never would have.

I was an adolescent. Not just literally, but my worldview, my understanding. In those years, I was really unable to conceive of what had gone into their relationship, the source of their commitment, the exquisite balance; things were so simple to me, clear-cut: "Just leave him," I'd say to George, wide-eyed, sincere. George was very patient with me. He knew, I think, that when you're young, you imagine there is endless time, opportunity, possibility—that you may invent any kind of life. George, ten years or so older than I, was more concerned with living the life he had. But he never said one condescending word to me, never rolled his eyes at my naïveté or my absurd (and often drunken) points of view.

And I've been looking at the picture of Ken, and one beside it of the two of them. Recalling the nasty things I used to say about Ken—"He's such a bore"; "He's pretty but not one-tenth as smart as you, George"; "He complains a lot"; "He's so demanding and you're always fighting, and you seem so unhappy all the time"; "All your friends just hate him, George"; "George, I'd get rid of him." These glossy prints in frames tell me that we are always quick to assess and judge couplings and marriages; but no one can ever know what was between these two men, the ways in which they were so right for each other. The private stuff—shared prayers and feeling loved, crying in one another's arms, the slamming doors followed by sweet, apologetic presents. Love. Love is bravery. . . .

I will keep that truth in mind when I am shamelessly berating that husband of yours, questioning your sanity for being with such a useless brute. Bert must mean something to you.

(Maybe I've never really loved.)

I'm dying to talk to George tomorrow, tell him I'm here. Cindy does not really count as company, at least not yet. She's curled on a rug by the door and snorts once in a while. George told me it would take a little time for Cindy to get adjusted to me—she's twelve years old, some kind of cranky terrier, tan-and-white. She's tolerating me, temporarily and conditionally allowing me to enact the master role; but she's clearly dispirited, not at all loyal, certainly not loving.

An hour later—

A dog, a book, a fire. Cuddled up in a wooden cabin, right by the ocean. Doesn't this scene seem so cozy? But suddenly I notice I've been holding my breath.

I'm scared here, Meg. God, the wind. And the silence, and the simplicity, the foreignness. The aloneness. I really have organized my life with so much business and rushing and need, fueled it with people, talk, food. At home, in the city, time comes in hours. Life is measured and crowded. A class. A meeting. A fight. Flirting with a student. Drinks, or a party, or a show, or a fuck.

Here, time is only air and light. Dawn, morning, day, twilight, evening, night. Night. Scary night.

Remember huddling under that enormous rolltop desk of Dad's at night, because we heard spooky sounds? They got mad at us for that, didn't they? They yelled and said we were acting like children. But we were children.

Here I am Meg—unaccountably sad. Safe, but not feeling safe. Settled, but feeling lost.

6

Dear Meg,

I'm starting my letter to you all over again. I actually fell asleep with the pen in my hand and my notebook on my chest. Such an eerie panic struck me last night, of loneliness and . . . identity, I guess. In this new place, away from all the people and things and habits I know, who am I? It was nighttime, and I can get so serious at night. And I don't want to alarm you or depress you. I don't want you to think I'm just nuts, Meg. . . .

It's summer; but, don't forget, seasons are different in California. Days are sunny, but brisk and fresh; and the fog settles in the early evening and it is actually quite chilly. George's house is right on the ocean—above it really, perched on a narrow, crooked cliff. From the porch I can see a few other houses, but mostly sea. A dirt road comes near the house, and across it is a pine forest.

Today I took my cameras and walked down the road a few yards, then followed a descending rocky path. In the distance, trees, bent from decades, maybe centuries, of brutal wind, covered the hillside, seeming to point toward the sky. Tough yellow and purple flowers, tall golden reeds, wild grass and brush lined a trail that seemed sometimes to end and then magically was visible again. I maneuvered under or over fallen dead trees, feeling exactly like a little boy, exploring the woods. I trudged around for three hours, Meg. I realized it was precisely this feeling I have come up here to know. Today satisfied a longing I've had for many years, and not even been aware of: to have mud on my shoes, and red cheeks, legs stinging from prickly shrubs. I have wanted to be out of breath, tripping over branches. I have needed to feel lost and disoriented, nervous and excited; and then to pick a direction, find a familiar spot.

I made my way up a steep incline, sliding back in the clay and pebbles, catching hold of a tree limb and pulling myself fully to the top. A clearing, from which I could see green all around, a peaceful, enveloping terrain. And then the sea, smashing itself in curls of white against inviolate black boulders.

This is Paradise. Stunning, mesmerizing. The vision is an ancient beauty. But the sounds are what really formed my sensation, as intense as anything sexual or religious, as inspiring as hatred or love.

I listened, just stood and listened. Above me, the bellow of dauntless wind through tall pines; beneath my feet, a whisper of reckless life scurrying deep inside the sand; out there, the roar of the surf against the shore. So loud, so loud, that there was only silence. My own breathing seemed soft, but it was really fast, full, content.

Of course, I had been clunking along for these hours with cameras hanging across my chest and wearing dark glasses, smoking cigarettes. Am I a paradox? Here is Nature, and then I intrude? That can't be; I am nature, too. Accidentally, without calculation, I had worn a white shirt and white pants, and so I was a stranger-angel today, making my awed, awkward progress, listening to this wild, thrilling stillness.

I'm in love, Meg. That's it. This peace comes when one is in love. I'm in love with this fresh air, this new territory. And I do feel loved in return.

Lovingly (and harmoniously),
Paul

7

"It's a dangerous world, Russell," Jane told her son. The two were stretched out on their backs in front of the dying coals in the fireplace grate. They shared a wool afghan. "Because anything can happen to you. Everything is chance. Everything is up to fate. You think I wanted to spend my whole life in this little town, Russell? After Mama died, after everyone had gone? That I wanted to stay here?"

"I don't know," answered Russell.

"You're goddamn right I didn't."

Between them was a bowl half filled with chocolate candies wrapped in silver foil. Russell reached into the bowl, pushed his sticky small fingers around, and took out three pieces.

"I had some pretty big plans, Russell." She sat up now and hugged her knees. She lit a cigarette, tossed the match onto the grate. "I was thinking about San Francisco. Ellen went to San Francisco. Ellen went to law school, even though everyone always said I was the really smart one. *I* could have been a lawyer in San Francisco. And Jesse got married to some rich guy. Somewhere. I don't know. A rich guy somewhere. And even Lucille got out of this town. Lucille's a dyke, but she's happy, she's been with the same woman all these years. They run some kind of a store or something."

Russell took another candy. "What is that? A lawyer?"

"It's someone who . . . someone who goes to court. Someone who defends people who are accused of crimes." Jane always was irritable when Russell asked her to define a word, and her explanations invariably would include other words Russell did not know.

" 'Accused'? What's 'accused'?"

Jane sat erect, pushed her spread fingers through her hair, not looking at the boy, trying to conceal her frustration. " 'Accused' is when someone says someone else did something bad." She could sense his puzzlement. She felt she could not bear another question. "Accused. Like if I go tell the police that you stole something." Now she turned to face Russell. "Do you see?"

Russell, lying on his back, giggled softly, crossed his arms over his chest. "But I didn't steal something," he said. "I didn't steal something, Jane."

"Well, if you take one more of those candies, I really will go tell the police." She roughly pulled the blanket up over her son's shoulder. She did not have patience for Russell, for his questions and interruptions. She'd not been thinking about words and candies. She'd been thinking about how dangerous the world is, and had been trying to teach her boy. Anything can happen. You can be eating a piece of chicken and choke on the bone. You can be standing on a street corner, about to mail a letter, and a truck will swerve and knock you down, or a lightning bolt will pierce your skull. You can be having a picnic lunch on the beach one day, but the tide can come and wash you away. And diseases. One day, as had happened to her mother, you wake up and nothing works. Legs are stiff, arms are sore, hair is brittle. You're very, very old. You cannot move. You're dying.

Russell was asleep in moments. His lips and fingers were stained with chocolate; his closed eyes were still. "There is no God," she told her sleeping son. "My mother thought there was a God. And the girls thought so. And they all said I was crazy, because I did not believe. They all said I should have faith, and I said why? Where? What kind? How? I called the girls stupid"—Jane laughed bitterly at her memory—"and Mama would get so sad. Don't fight, girls, don't fight, girls. Quoting things from the Bible as she laid there in that bed. Couldn't even sip some water on her own. Crying that there must be a God."

She was silent for some moments. If I hear any footsteps near my house, Jane was thinking, I'll get my shotgun. I always had to wear Ellen's old shoes, Jane was remembering. The walk in front of the house used to have tiny pots of marigolds lining it; what happened to those marigolds? She had liked a boy in school once, but the boy was scared of Jane's sick mother.

"Well, Russell," she said too loudly to her sleeping son. "There is no God."

When it was dark outside, and the oil lamp was burning low, Jane woke Russell. She led him up the stairs, and he stumbled, for he was still so sleepy. She secured him in his bed and stood over him. She thought about kissing him on the cheek or on the forehead. But she didn't do it.

8

Dear Meg—

I just finished a simple supper: salad and soup and nice bread. I did try to phone George today. When I walked in the lobby of the hotel (called the Hotel Universe, if you can believe that), an excruciatingly handsome, dark-haired, hazel-eyed bellboy directed me to the telephone booth as if he were showing me to their grandest suite; they must not have many guests in the place. It is a charming old inn with maroon carpets and mahogany walls and an enormous, empty dining room.

I dialed a number George had given me, but got a recording that said the line was temporarily out of service. I called back; same recording. Then I reached the university and was put on hold and switched from line to line. I finally asked if I could leave a message, and the receptionist loudly cracked her gum as she took the information. I'm very prejudiced against gum-cracking receptionists, so I hardly expected my message to reach George. Then, an hour or so later, I walked back down the hill to place the call again. Now there was no recording, just a ring, which I listened to absently, leaning against the glass wall of the booth.

The bellboy watched me from a few feet away, standing with his hands behind his back, chin up, back straight. I clumsily left the booth.

"Can't reach your friend?" the bellboy asked helpfully.

"No, no," I stammered. "I can't understand it. I'll try again tomorrow." I left the place with my head lowered, as though I'd been caught doing something wrong.

I had tied Cindy's leash to a parking meter, and because it was a cool evening, I decided to roam around the town a bit. No street lamps, only silver-gray glows from windows here and there, eerily suspended in the dark. The feel of the steady, pleasing wind—the sound of it. I wish I could take pictures of what I hear.

When I was nearly back to George's place, I stopped and looked down the road at that old house, the one where the woman and the boy live. It is mostly hidden by some trees and an ugly complex of metal towers with wires and conductors; but I could make out a dilapidated porch, the edge of the roof, and one lighted window. I stepped a foot or two closer to the house, and noticed that Cindy's leash was pulled taut; she had sat down, facing away, back toward town. I tugged, but she wouldn't budge. I stood for a few minutes, with my hands tucked in my jacket pockets. I saw no movement inside the house, heard nothing. Then I felt lonely, somehow; as though something were just out of my reach. Unrequitedness.

God, Meg—so much thinking up here. I didn't expect this inwardness, this reflection. Because I'm not chattering and laughing and gossiping and drinking. Or pontificating about photography—worse, pontificating about art. I came up here to relax, to take some deep breaths, to calm down a bit. But now, isolated, my normal self seems silly to me. Silly? No—strained, false. Here, I am subjected to a rhythm of moods. Here, suddenly, my brain's in snarls and scrambles. I am panicked (and know it's crazy) about not being able to reach George. Also, I have a feeling I am being watched.

And then, too, thoughts of Mark. His terrible last days. Fast melancholy. The real me is leaking out and it is . . . I don't know what. Childish, I was going to say. Very happy for an hour, and the next hour, very sad. That's what I remember of childhood.

I will look out the window and see the sea breeze pushing the branches of a giant weeping willow. And then think of us. When we were kids, Meg. You and me in new *clothes for Easter, shiny shoes. You hated your white gloves and hair ribbon. You hated the little purse they made you carry. You smiled, but you hated it.*

I had a navy blue suit with short pants and a red bow tie. Did I hate Easter, too, Meg? I can't remember what I felt. I can't remember what I felt.

Write soon,
Paul

PART II

I

Jane stood at the window, behind Dr. Landau's desk. Through lavender venetian blinds she could see her Pontiac in the parking lot, and a few other cars, and a supermarket across the two-lane highway. "We liked the other clinic better," said Jane. "This one is too modern. We liked Dr. Lynch, didn't we, Russell?" She turned to Russell, who was sitting on a leather armchair with a picture book open on his lap.

"Dr. Lynch," Russell repeated flatly, and rubbed his eye with his knuckle.

"Dr. Lynch had to retire." Jane slid her finger along the spines of some medical books on a shelf. "Because he was old. And that's why we come here to this lady doctor." On Dr. Landau's desk was a framed photograph; Jane bent down to get a better look. There were two children, and a man with glasses, and Dr. Landau, smiling, wearing a yellow dress. "This must be an old picture," Jane said. "Her hairstyle is out of date. I don't like it."

The door was opened; Dr. Landau stepped inside, walked briskly across the room, and for a moment the two women were both behind the desk, facing each other. The doctor wore her white lab coat; the end of a stethoscope hung from the pocket. Jane wore her black dress, black stockings, flat shoes. Jane's black beret was slanted on her head, nearly covering one ear.

"Good morning, Jane. Sorry to have kept you waiting. Why don't you have a seat?" and the doctor nodded at a chair.

"That's all right, Doctor. I'm glad you could fit me in. I know it was last-minute." Jane sat beside Russell.

Dr. Landau seated herself in the desk chair and opened a file folder before her. The doctor's glasses had large, oval frames with thick lenses. "Well, I was surprised to see you, Jane. You brought Russell in—when was it?" She moved her finger down a page in the file. "Three weeks ago. And I'd seen Russell—yes, I'd seen him just two weeks before that."

"I know that, Dr. Landau. But Russell—something serious is going on."

"Serious?"

"Yes, his symptoms are getting worse."

"What symptoms, Jane?" the doctor asked, and held her pen, ready to write.

Jane moved a bit of hair away from her face with two fingers. "Okay. First of all, I think he's having hearing problems. Sometimes it looks like he's listening to me, but then he doesn't respond. So I'm concerned about that. And in the morning, when he wakes up, I see a strange kind of spot on his pillow—"

"A spot?"

"A stain. I think it's a discharge from his ear."

"What color is this stain?"

"Yellow. A yellowish color."

Dr. Landau wrote down what she'd been told. "And are there other symptoms, Jane?"

"Diarrhea."

"Diarrhea," repeated the doctor, writing. "How long has that been going on?"

"A week at least."

"I see." Dr. Landau removed her glasses, pinched the bridge of her nose with her thumb and forefinger.

"You look tired," Jane said, too softly.

"Excuse me?" The doctor replaced her glasses.

"I didn't say anything."

"Has there been anything else?"

"Well, I've also noticed a rash on his scalp, under his hair. I can't tell what it is, I keep looking at it."

"Is it uncomfortable?" asked the doctor.

"Uncomfortable?"

"Yes. Does it itch?"

"I—I don't know," answered Jane. She looked down then, her gaze falling absently on a corner of the desk.

"Well, is Russell scratching his scalp? Does this rash appear to be bothering *him?*" Now Dr. Landau seemed annoyed, impatient.

"He doesn't complain," Jane said quickly.

"Fine," said the doctor. She rose abruptly, extended her hand, the palm flat. "Come with me, Russell. Let's have a look."

The boy slid down from the leather chair and joined the doctor, took her hand. The two left the office and went into an examining room across the hall. Jane was alone. Jane was thinking: She should have some magazines in here. For the parents who are waiting and nervous and anxious. She could at least have some magazines.

Jane was remembering that Dr. Lynch, who was a man and old, had always let her in the room when he examined Russell. She remembered Dr. Lynch shining a light in Russell's ear, a light in his eye. Feeling the boy's chest. Knocking the knees with a rubber mallet. But this lady doctor had said she preferred to see the children alone, it was better for the children.

Jane rose, walked to the shelf of books. All the bindings were the same; it was a series of medical texts. *Pediatrics.* Jane stood before the shelf, lightly touching the spines of the books with the tips of two fingers. "Doctor," she whispered, "can I borrow some of these books, would that be all right?" She pulled out one of the books. She opened to the table of contents and rifled through pages of charts and footnotes and drawings. Stealthily, swiftly, Jane slid the volume into her giant bag, then folded it closed.

The door was opened and Jane turned around. Russell and the doctor walked in and each took a seat.

"Well," said Dr. Landau, "for the diarrhea, let me suggest some white rice and unbuttered toast."

"Yes, I've been doing that," Jane said.

"Fine."

"And I don't think it's working."

"Well, keep it up, Jane. It *will* work. Maybe a little ripe banana, too. You like banana, don't you, Russell?" she asked the child, and she smiled. Then she looked at Jane. "Now, about his ears. I see nothing wrong with Russell's ears. Could be a little cleaner, but nothing wrong at all. And I've looked at Russell's scalp, Jane, and I do not see any rash. No flaking or redness. Nothing."

"No, I know that," Jane said, defensive, impatient. "Sometimes it disappears, it looks fine, and then it comes back, just as suddenly."

Dr. Landau closed the file folder. She leaned forward, her elbows on her desk. "That sounds very unusual. I haven't heard of anything like that before."

"I think—"

"Yes?"

"Would it be all right if I called you by your first name? Florence?"

"Of course."

"Because you call me by my first name."

"That would be perfectly fine. Now. What I suggest is the rice and toast and banana. I suggest you give the office a call next week and let us know how everything's going." Dr. Landau stood up. She had her fingers spread apart, as though the surface of her desk were a piano and she was getting ready to play the scales.

Jane rose too. She took Russell's hand. "Shouldn't I bring him in? Shouldn't we make an appointment so you can see him again?"

"No, Jane. Russell will do just fine. Unless anything out of the ordinary happens, I just want you to call us next week. Do you understand?"

Jane and Russell walked to the office door. Dr. Landau was behind them. "I'd feel more comfortable if I brought him back in," Jane said. She did not appear particularly anxious; she seemed cross, dissatisfied.

"Jane?"

Jane turned around. "Yes, Florence?"

Dr. Landau stepped closer to Jane, spoke softly so the boy would not hear. "Jane, it isn't good to make too much of a fuss about every little thing. It's not good for your son. Do you understand, Jane?"

Jane was stunned. She was offended. She considered saying nothing in reply, simply turning and leaving that clinic. And then writing a letter to Dr. Landau. But she answered, speaking in a low tone as the doctor had done: "Of course I understand, Florence."

Dr. Landau smiled and placed a hand on Jane's arm, and Jane started, winced. "Bye-bye, then," said the doctor. "And bye-bye to you, Russell."

Russell laughed, lifting his head up to look at the lady. Jane and Russell walked down a corridor. Jane heard the doctor step back into her office and the door close.

The nurse at the clinic's reception desk was a black woman. Jane felt relieved. She trusted black people more than white people. Jane thought, and had told Russell many times, that black people were smarter and had bigger hearts than white people. Jane told the nurse: "Yes, Dr. Landau wants to see my little boy next week. Early in the week. She asked me to make an appointment with you."

"Certainly," the nurse said and opened a notebook.

"Sometimes," Jane told the nurse, "these rare childhood diseases are very hard to keep under control."

"Oh, I'm sure that's true." The nurse wrote Jane's name on a schedule in pencil. "Tuesday all right?" she asked.

"Nothing earlier?"

"I'm afraid not. No, Tuesday's the soonest."

"Well, that will have to do. Listen, I have a question for you."

"Yes?"

"Is Dr. Landau Jewish?"

"Is she—is she Jewish?" The nurse was shocked at the question, seemed as though she thought it was a joke. And then she could see it was not a joke, and she frowned. She was disconcerted. She looked down at her desk and moved some papers from one side to the other. "You'd have to—you'd have to ask the doctor that, I think."

2

Dear Meg:

Got your letter. I have a teacher's assistant (who claims he's bisexual) forwarding all of my mail from school. Thanks for the pictures. Audrey has grown into a very eccentric-looking child—weird, I'd even say—which I love. You look too thin and exhausted, though. I'm worried about you. Bert, as usual, looks sullen. I admit my opinion of your husband is very much influenced by Mother. She's mostly bothered because Bert can't hold a job; that is not my objection. I'm concerned because you two don't seem happy together: he gives you grief, diminishes your life rather than enriching it. I might be off the track. We live so far away from each other, Meg, and all I see are a couple of snapshots. And your smile seems strained, your eyes seem angry. There's love in your hands though, holding your baby's shoulders sweetly, firmly. And Bert looks . . . well . . . sullen. (Mind my own business?)

Are you serious that you're still buying all those lottery tickets?

So I've been up here about a week and a half. Seems like all summer. The colors are so vibrant, unbelievably rich—one tree will offer every possible shade of green and yellow and gray and brown, like some painter imagined it. I've been shooting in black-and-white, to isolate the shapes, to make shadows, to try and define this wild landscape apart from its color. On today's walk, I had that vicious Cindy with me. She is so disobedient. She'll suddenly stop, sit down, stare miserably ahead of her. No coaxing or threats can budge her. And sometimes she goes too far ahead and I call her name; I know she hears, because her ears shoot back, but she waddles forward petulantly.

The strangest thing is that I still can't reach George. I've been back to the Hotel Universe phone booth three or four times and something always prevents me from getting George on the phone: he's just left or he's in class, and once I was even disconnected.

I have been seeing Ancer Peak around town quite a bit. He is more than odd—sometimes he will greet me and make his blithe, unspecific offer of having me over; but sometimes he passes me by, as though we've never met. Finally, I noticed him sitting in his car (a yellow convertible) and went up to him, thinking he might have a clue about George.

"I can't reach him," I said.

Ancer Peak said: "Well, don't get hysterical." (I was not hysterical, and resented that characterization.) "He'll turn up." Then he invited me up to his house for cocktails. Though I could tell he was a fairly predictable little queen, I found myself grateful for the attention. I stopped home to change and found myself sincerely bewildered about what to wear; then regretting that I'd agreed to go. He makes me tense, that little man, and I can't even understand why. I only know I don't trust Ancer Peak.

I am needing someone I can really tell of my experience here—of these walks through the woods, of the isolation and beauty. There are dead, silver-gray trees outside my house; when they are blown by the wind, they make a sound like creaky floorboards, so scary when you're a child. My time here has been all sensation and flashes of memory; every moment is profound, but elusive also, indecipherable. Something meaningful is in front of me. Does that make sense? I hope it does make sense to you. You have become, like it or not, my listener.

Anyway—Ancer Peak's house is laid out much more handsomely and richly than George's. He must have thrown a fortune into the place. Ancer Peak is not up here to be rustic. Everything's shiny blond wood; colorful woolen blankets are tossed over handsome, comfortable chairs; there is a giant fireplace and a completely modern kitchen. Also, television and a stereo system. And, of course, his piano.

He'd laid out several impeccably rolled joints and a bottle of wine with glasses, and we settled deep into pastel-green cushions on the forest-green sofa. "Just some water or soda for me," I said, and Ancer Peak was visibly disappointed, even a little disapproving.

"Anyway, so how are you liking our little town?" he asked with forced politeness.

"The town? The town—I don't really know much about it. I go over to Moxie's for food and to get my mail. I stroll through now and then. I've mostly been walking out the other way, past the highway, into the woods and along the cliffs and beach."

"You're a photographer, George told me," said Ancer Peak, sipping, but keeping his crossed eyes fixed in my general direction. Here, my monstrous pride was pricked: I am a fairly famous photographer, after all. A résumé of my museum and gallery credits and published articles and books maniacally floated through my consciousness. But, as I usually do when I'm full of conceit and pretension, I responded quite humbly, saying only: "Oh, yes."

"Well, it's certainly a picturesque little place," Ancer Peak declared. "I would think it would be just scrumptious for photographs. Beautiful scenery." Now, I've noticed that Ancer Peak speaks in an English accent; I should say "affects" one, for it is inconsistent, it lapses occasionally. Why would someone put on a bogus accent?

"Now, for someone writing a novel," he went on, "it would really be a gold mine. The characters in this place. I've been up here, on and off, for ten years now, so people are pretty used to me. But generally—and you should keep this in mind, Paul—there's a certain hostility for the city folk." He lighted one of his joints, inhaled deeply. Holding his breath, his eyes reddening, he offered it to me and I shook my head, smiling ingenuously. Ancer Peak exhaled. "That's the thing: city versus town. Oh, they're simple, they're sweet. It's just that they've lived here all their lives, they're not sophisticated. Up in the hills you'll find some hippie types. They make clay pots and grow weed and play guitars. Terribly boring. And further out"—he waved his hand at the enormous window, to indicate some area away from us—"there's been some building. City people setting up weekend retreats. And the town people like the money, naturally, but they still have a . . . a kind of a judgment. You know?" Here he burst into an unattractive, phlegmatic laugh, which startled me. "God knows what they say about me behind my back." So I laughed, too.

And then we were silent for some moments. Ancer Peak's shelves were full of beautifully bound books. A very impressive range, actually: Nietzsche, James, Freud, Aristotle and Plato, Shakespeare, Dostoevsky, Gide and Mann and Kafka. And there were several James Joyce shelves, the fiction, some studies and biographies. I said: "Oh, you're a James Joyce enthusiast."

"Came across this the other day," Ancer Peak said, leaning forward. "Do you know what Virginia Woolf said of James Joyce?"

I shook my head.

"That she considered Ulysses *the work of an undergraduate scratching at his pimples. Isn't that hysterical?"*

Then I said—and it was an uncritical, barely-thought-out observation: "You don't seem to have any books by women."

"Women?" He said the word incredulously, as though I'd remarked that he had no books by frogs.

"Well, I was just noticing it—" I tried to explain.

"But, like who? Like what women?"

"What women?" Now I was incredulous. Was he was joking? "Of course you're familiar with women writers."

"Name some."

I had the names—dozens of names, from Cather to McCullers to Sontag to the Brontës to Porter, Stein, George Sand, Welty, O'Connor and poets and essayists. This was absurd.

"Well, Virginia Woolf," I said.

"Touché, darling. You've got me there."

I rose. I meandered around the room, glancing at framed drawings on the walls, little vases and boxes placed deliberately on well-dusted surfaces. I could feel him watching me, hear him sip his drink occasionally, sense his creepy smugness. I knew I did not want to see him again. It's funny, because he is just the kind of person I would gossip and joke with at home; as a rule I have great affection for rude queens and feel the most fundamental kind of alliance with them, like we are related by blood and understand each other. But now I felt alienated, awkward. I was planning an exit line.

And it was as though Ancer Peak sensed my restlessness. He asked: "Have you met Jane yet?"

"Jane?"

"You've seen her, probably. She has a little boy." Ancer Peak's tone, maybe, gave me some sort of vague understanding that Jane was someone I needed to know about.

I felt blackmailed. I grabbed a cigarette from the pack on the coffee table and took my seat.

"She's the legend of the town. She's crazy. You know how every small town has a crazy lady?"

"What's crazy about her?"

"Now, that I don't really know. Not the source of it. Legends have a momentum of their own. I know that she's extremely unpleasant when it comes to my piano-playing. She used to send me notes, saying that I was interrupting her studies (God knows what those are), and keeping her little boy awake. She's lived there all her life, right there in that same house. It's down the road, not far from you, right on the rocks. All the town children are afraid of her; they make up little stories and rhymes and things. Her boy is Russell—a scandal, my dear, because she's never been married and no one knows who Russell's father is."

"Is the little boy sick?"

"Sick?"

I did not know why I'd asked such a question. I was stunned, because the thought had so suddenly entered my mind, the words had seemed to escape from me, not as though I was inquiring about crazy Jane—more like I was uncontrollably disclosing something about myself.

"Sick?" mused Ancer Peak, exhaling a cone of gray smoke. "No, I haven't heard that he's sick. He's about six now. He's supposed to be in school, but the rumor is that Jane refuses to send him. She's had some fights with the school officials. I don't know. The public school is far away, so town people send their kids to the Methodist school here. Well, Jane won't have her son to say grace before he gets his cookies and milk. That's what she's like."

She sounded perfectly sensible to me, but I said nothing.

Ancer said: "I know if the kid ever does get to school, the other kids will crucify him. Kids can be so cruel."

Ancer Peak poured some more wine for himself and settled cozily against the cushions on the sofa. "All I know is, one night I had a few friends over, people visiting up from the city. This was last year some time. And we were singing and carrying on, a little loud, I'm sure, but this was a Saturday night, my dear, not Sunday morning. And then we all heard this loud boom. We all froze. What was that? What was that? Then it came again. You know what it was? It was that sick Jane, down the hill, shooting her shotgun into the air. Can you imagine?"

By this time I could hardly tolerate Ancer Peak at all—his giddy, self-satisfied tone. He's a fake. It is as though every phrase is being performed. So I thanked him for

inviting me over, said I wished I could stay longer but that I was suddenly very sleepy.
I was going on about how early in the morning I've been getting up, but Ancer Peak
was not the least bit interested. He hopped up and showed me to the door, would not
look at me. He behaved as though I'd been unconscionably rude to him, and I felt sorry
and worried; but, as I walked down the hill I realized with some irritation that he
was the rude one. It was already dark. I passed out on the bed, not even fully undressed.
And now, really confounded, I'm wondering: Why can't I reach George?

Love from your "hysterical" brother,
Paul

3

"Two kinds of people in the world," Jane was telling her son, and she
had said this to him many times before. "There's the kind who always
get things their way. Everything works out for them. These are the
lucky ones. Then there's the unlucky ones: the kind who always lose."
She was at the kitchen table, her legs crossed, smoking a cigarette.

Russell sat across from her with the things from his special box laid
out on the oilcloth: markers, string, crayons, and paper. A frantic green
circle he'd drawn delighted him and he pushed the paper toward his
mother. "This is that big tree outside."

Jane looked at the drawing, exhaled smoke. "It doesn't look like a
tree to me, Russell. It looks like a messy squiggle. Did you finish—
Russell, you didn't finish all that rice I made for you." The boy had
pushed his plate off to the side, and Jane now pushed it back before
him. "No more drawing or anything like that until you finish that rice.
The doctor said."

Russell frowned. He blinked sleepily. "I'm full, Jane."

"You hardly touched it at all."

The boy's frown deepened, his brow tensed.

"Now don't you cry, Russell. You eat that rice." Jane picked up his
fork and put it in his hand, wrapped his fingers into a fist around it.

Russell lifted a bit of rice to his lips and pushed it onto his tongue. His expression was one of distaste, of distrust; and there were tears in his eyes, but he did not blink and the tears stood still. Jane lit another cigarette. She crossed the kitchen and poured herself some coffee from the brown pot on the stove. "It's for his own good," Jane said, aloud. "He's mad at me, he thinks I'm being mean. But it's for his own good."

A little bit of daylight disappeared with every strained bite Russell took of his white rice. Jane sat at the table; she washed a pot and rinsed the glasses; she leaned against the counter. She smoked and tapped cigarette ash into her hand, then shook the ash into the sink. The rice was getting colder, too, and stickier. "You must be eating that rice one little kernel at a time," Jane declared, standing now at the screen door, facing out into the evening. "That piano again," she muttered as some jazzy tune filtered through the cool night. "One day I'll burn that man's house to the ground.

"Finally," she said loudly, and swept his plate and fork from the table. Russell leaned back in his chair wearily.

"I've got you a present, Russell." Jane hurried to her bag on the counter, and out of it she brought a stack of seven or eight paper cups. "I took these today from the water cooler at the clinic," she explained, bringing them to the table, seating herself across from him. "These are for you to make things out of. You see? You can make little houses"—she placed a couple of the cups on the table—"or you could make a tower of a castle." She balanced one cup atop the other two. "Oh, is Russell mad at Jane? Is Russell so mad at Jane because she makes him eat his rice?" Jane's tone was sharp, penetrating, almost mean.

"No," said the boy, very softly, drawing out the sound of the word and keeping his lips in the "O" shape.

"Or you know what else?" She leaned closer, her elbows on the table, holding one of the paper cups. "We can make masks." Jane placed the cup over her nose and sat erect. "See? Make some little whiskers and I'm a cat. Or draw a little beak and I'm a bird. And then we can tie the mask over your head and—"

"I don't feel good."

Jane rose abruptly. She went to Russell and placed her palm against his forehead, then touched her fingers to his throat. "You feel cold, Russell. Cold to the touch."

*   *   *

Jane came home at dawn. She eased her car over the uneven, rocky drive and turned off the motor. A neighborhood cat landed on the hood of her car. Jane tapped two fingers gently against the windshield; the cat stared, then fled. She knew all the cats and would feed them when they came to her porch.

She remembered cats fighting—the scary, crazy screeching. She remembered a siren from an ambulance. She remembered her mother standing in a doorway, some doorway, crying and red-faced.

In her kitchen, she lighted an oil lamp and sat wearily at the table. She leaned back so the wooden chair rested on two legs. Jane removed the tie from her hair so that it fell loose around her shoulders. She placed her hands flat on her thighs, firmly at first, then gently. She rocked in her creaky chair and closed her eyes. She'd had beer tonight. She was tense and tired and mad. Jane had not slept, and now it was nearly daylight, and soon Russell would wake up. She slid her fingers gently between her legs. She held her hands flat together, like praying hands, and pushed them against the stiff material of her baggy man's trousers. She rocked in the chair, pushed her praying hands against herself.

Give me strength give me strength give me strength. But was she saying these words, or only thinking them? Was she shouting out or whispering or only breathing the words? Give me strength. At the bar tonight, some drunken man had asked her what was on her mind. She told him nothing that was on her mind was any of his business. The drunken man said she was a tough one, wasn't she?

She rocked the chair. She unbuttoned her old sweater and it fell from her shoulders, away from her breasts, slid to the floor. She quickly undid the fly of the trousers and pulled them down to her knees. She closed her praying hands, lacing the fingers, pressing them tight so the knuckles were white. Some phony blond woman tonight had blown smoke in Jane's face and Jane had told her not to ever blow smoke in her face again. The phony blond woman laughed and then asked Jane if she were a man or a woman? Are you a man or a woman? Then looked to the bartender, asked the bartender, Is this a man or a woman?

Naked and alone at dawn, Jane curled her hands and pressed hard against herself, pushing to get up inside herself, turning her knuckles in tiny, swift circles. Give me strength give me strength. Now it was like an order. Jane was not one to plead or hope; she demanded.

She cried out when she felt herself rising, when she felt the heat and wetness. She cried out, "God," like she'd been punched. Then she breathed fully, leaned back her head, wiped her fingers on her neck and throat. Some girl, long ago, had laughed at Jane and said, Your neck is funny, your neck is too long, you look like a giraffe. So everyone called her Giraffe for a while.

Tender, spent, angry. She pulled up her trousers and fastened them; she wrapped the sweater tightly around herself. Daylight had come, through gray fog which would lift in the next hours. She was quick about laying out Russell's breakfast—juice, toast, a piece of melon. She brewed some coffee for herself. When she put down the plates and silverware, she did it roughly, carelessly, and the butter dish got chipped.

She heard those birds. They gathered, only in the morning, flew from the top of the pine tree to the wires, where they formed a line. Back to their tree, then they swooped and soared, singing. Singing louder the higher they flew. And then they were out of sight, but Jane could still hear them. She remembered one of her sisters telling her, long ago, when Jane was just a little girl: Those are the larks, Jane. Those are larks singing.

4

Dear Meg:

Sorry to hear about Bert. I got the news from Mother. I called her yesterday from the famous Hotel Universe pay phone, and she told me of his series of disasters. She was remarkably toneless—you know how she can be—so it was a matter of listening between the lines. He had a car accident, but he's not hurt. (Between the lines: he'd been drinking.) And he did not get that computer job. (Between the lines: he didn't try very hard.) Mother ends the conversation: "Well, I'm sure they'll work things out." And between those lines is judgment and anger, resignation and distance.

I'm doing well here. It's been wet this week. The rain comes, then retreats, like army troops. Finally sunny today, though. I have brought Cindy down the cliff—practically dragging her, for it is steep—and have spent the better part of the day on the beach. It's not the beach of our childhood: crowded and white, smelling of fish and suntan oil. This one's a narrow strip of dirty sand. A floor of pebbles and a wall of gray rocks blocks the surf. It's a rough place, strewn with bird feathers and beer cans. It's a majestic place, too. Across the bay are ranges of brown and green hills and low, still clouds.

I'm leaning back against a rock, watching the waves, holding a stupid detective novel closed on my lap. My camera is by my side. I'm peaceful, Meg. Which is something I've not known before. Restlessness, greed, worry, ecstasy—these are familiar. Hunting and racing and waiting, singing loud, laughing loud. Pouting and yelling. Here I am calmly and deeply and simply breathing. I am peaceful.

Cindy has been at the water's edge, growling, in a contest with the tide. When the foamy water line comes too close, she barks. I just spent a moment watching her shit. Carefully balanced, but swaying slightly, her back legs spread, the front legs in close, her butt suspended, and the most intense expression on her mean little face: dignified, concentrating. As the shit plopped in two easy links, Cindy's legs trembled, her ears went back flat.

I want sex! (Is this appropriate to say to one's sister? And, God, what is the sick psychology that makes the thought arise, and so urgently, while I'm watching a crapping dog?) Well, I won't go into explicit detail. Just that there's a young guy stretched out flat fifty yards or so from me. Is he naked? No, he has on some skimpy denim shorts. His hair is so blond it looks white, his skin is orange-brown. He's been here maybe an hour, sunning and reading, sleeping, turning onto his back, then onto his front. I keep glancing over at him, but he doesn't look my way. Sexy and lazy and insouciant.

Later—still at the beach. The wind is stronger, the sun is reddening. I closed my eyes for some minutes. And when I opened them, my childhood was here. I could see you, Meg, in your yellow swimsuit, with your bony shoulders and knees, making your way across the sand carrying soda cans and hot dogs in a cardboard tray. I could see Dad, a triangle of white cream on his nose, sitting in a beach chair, wearing a hat, waving to you, waving to me, laughing because you jumped right on the sand castle we'd made—you, rebel. I could see Mother, lying still, huge sunglasses practically covering her face. She had a paperback book. She'd pushed the skinny straps of her suit off her shoulders. She would not notice us.

I can see you and Dad and Mother. I can see some kids with their mothers. Grandparents under umbrellas with picnic coolers. A man jogging with his dog. More kids and mothers and dogs. Some teenage boys with their radio on too loud. (Mother: "Those boys have their radio on too loud.") I can see plastic shovels and pails. I can see wood floating, just at the edge of the water. But I cannot see me. Where am I? Did I say I was peaceful? I'm not peaceful. Neither am I anxious or angry or even lonely. I don't know what I am—alienated, somehow, from what I am. A swell of a colder breeze, and the sun disappears behind clouds. The sunning youth seems not to notice or care about time or temperature, about me and this dog, or anything.

I'm ready to go. Come on, Cindy. Come Cindy. Let's leave here, let's go back. Come Cindy.

5

Russell was out there on the porch, barefooted, wearing overalls but no shirt, for the day was humid. Jane had set Russell to making animal masks from the paper cups and string. She held the phone receiver against her ear with her raised shoulder. Jane drew deeply on her cigarette, tossed it into the kitchen sink, and through a cloud of exhaled smoke said angrily: "Dr. *Landau.* I'm holding for Dr. Landau. I've *been* holding. Hello? Hello, Florence?"

"Yes, Jane. Good morning. How are you this morning?"

"Russell is not good. He's worse. I want to bring him in to see you."

"Jane, really. Since the last time you were here, you have called every single day. Twice a day sometimes."

Anxiously, Jane interrupted. "But Florence, listen, I've been doing some reading. I've been going through a pediatrics text."

"I see."

"Yes, and I think I've found some very strange symptoms that apply to Russell, that would explain everything that's wrong with Russell."

"That's just it, you see. There is nothing wrong with Russell."

"You've misdiagnosed him, Florence. Isn't that possible?"

"That I've misdiagnosed Russell?"

"Yes. Isn't that possible? That does happen, doesn't it? Doctors aren't perfect."

"Of course not. And it *would* be possible for me to misdiagnose Russell. Except that I have not diagnosed him at all. He has no symptoms. He has no illness." The doctor's tone was firm and even, controlled, concealing impatience. After a pause: "Do you understand? Jane, excuse me for a second; the nurse has a question. —What's that? Oh, yes, tell Mrs. Franklin I will need to schedule time with the surgeon, and give her the surgeon's card; tell her we will get back to her this afternoon.— Hello? Jane?"

"Yes, hello?"

"Pardon me, Jane. I'm back now."

"Dr. Landau?"

"Yes, Jane, I'm here."

"Some child is having surgery?"

"Yes. Tonsillectomy."

"Florence, Russell threw up last night. In his sleep. He was very cold to the touch; then he felt like he was burning up. And after he'd gone to sleep, he threw up."

"All right, Jane."

"And he is absolutely having problems with his hearing. I don't know why you can't see any problems when you look in his ears, because it is very obvious that he isn't hearing properly. I was reading all about this very rare condition, and it happens just at Russell's age. I can find it in this book."

"No, Jane. That won't be necessary."

"Oh, I hear some music in the background. What is that music?"

"It's Beethoven. Piano concerto on the radio."

"It's pretty. Florence? Florence, I know you think I'm overreacting. That I imagine things wrong with Russell."

"But you don't imagine it? It's really true? Russell really has all of these problems you say he has?"

"He does, Florence."

"Well, then, Jane, I suggest you take Russell to another pediatrician. I can give you some names if you'd like. My assessment of Russell's general health is that he is fine. I've asked him, Jane, about how he feels. If his ears bother him, if his stomach bothers him. Russell has no complaints."

"He's afraid, he's afraid to talk to anyone but me—"

The doctor continued: "Now, I'm not happy with the diet you give him. And I've told you that. I'm concerned also about his coloring, because I believe you do not let Russell play outside very often, certainly not often enough. He needs exercise and fresh air and I've told you that as well."

"You sound mad at me, Dr. Lynch."

"Dr. Landau, Jane. Dr. Lynch retired, you remember. I'm Dr. Landau. And I don't mean to be harsh. I'm not mad. But I feel it's time to be frank. You have brought Russell in to see me more times—I have examined Russell more in these past two months than I've examined some children through all of their school years. There's something wrong, Jane."

"There is something wrong. I know there's something wrong."

"I don't mean that. I don't mean that there's something wrong with your little boy. That is not what I mean. Jane? Are you there?"

"He needs me. Russell needs me. He's got some kind of disease. He could die."

"What? You think he's going to die?"

"What?"

"Jane, you said you thought Russell was going to die."

"I did not say that, Florence. That's not what I said."

"Listen, Jane. I'm sorry it hasn't worked out. My receptionist will give you a list of references, other doctors. You try them. You are entitled to have a doctor you trust, and it really seems that you do not trust me."

"Do you have children, Florence?"

"No. No, I don't."

"You had a child, but it died?"

"No, Jane. I've never had children."

"Ah. Then you're exempt."

"I don't know what you mean, Jane. I don't—I don't understand you. I'll give you to my receptionist, shall I? And she will help you in finding a doctor more suitable. All right, Jane? Jane?—She's still on the line. I can hear her. I can hear her breathing, but she won't answer—Hello? Jane?"

6

Dear Meg:

Won anything from the lottery yet?

I'm a little weary, finally. It's nearly three weeks I've been up here. My hair is longer than it's been in some years, curling over my collar. And I haven't shaved.

This landscape is still glorious: its freshness, its color, its huge, humbling brilliance. I remain intrigued especially by the sounds—elegant whispers from the wind, outrageous pounding from the sea, wild noises from birds and cats and dogs, even the unexplainable creaking of this old house. The sounds are so exquisite, as though they'd been composed and arranged.

And I have been keeping busy, shooting rolls and rolls of film. But thoughts of home have begun to creep in; no, not so much of home, but of myself at home, my other self, a person I know better and see more clearly. There's no particular friend I miss, no place I'm specifically longing for. I'm certainly not missing faculty meetings and classes.

But I'll be turning my lens to focus on a peculiar stand of yellow-green bent reeds, and all of a sudden a tune will hum inside my head—some smoky Billie Holiday ballad. And then I feel out of place. Someone left a day-old copy of the San Francisco Chronicle on a bench in the town square; the headline was about an indicted city official, the photo showed a sour-faced man being led away by police. I can't describe the feeling of remoteness I had when I saw that newspaper, and affection for all the big-city crooks and crises. I do feel intensely foreign here. Life and people and terrain are all of one kind, connected by their district, their history: they understand the world through each other.

"I saw her go out again last night," I heard an older man confiding to one of the ladies at Moxie's.

"No," was the lady's reply.

The man nodded. "That's right. Had to be about midnight because, well, you know I always go to bed just after the stroke of midnight."

She nodded; she did know that.

"That's right. Left in her car about midnight. And when do you think she came home?"

"No," the lady gasped, anticipating the shocking answer.

The man nodded. "That's right. Sunup. I was already awake and having my coffee and I looked out my pantry window. And in she drove."

The lady shook her head. My purchase of some postcards was irritating, trivial business to her. Probably they seemed odd things to buy, also. They were dusty on their rack. Postcards—because I don't belong here, and I'm sending them off to where I do belong, to real people.

In your letter to me, you said "the novelty of nature" would wear off. I guess you're right. I guess you know all about that, too. That what is sublimely fulfilling on a Tuesday, by Thursday can seem stifling. By Saturday, maybe it's tragic.

I don't know what to say about the new developments with Bert. I liked to make jokes about him, I really did think he was (as Mother says) a "ne'er-do-well." But this . . . I assume if you'd wanted to go into details with me, you would have. I won't push. "This is it, Paul, the last straw," you wrote. I did not even really know there had been so many straws. "He hit me," you wrote, and that was all. Your words were stinging and told enough. I cried reading them, Meg. Will she be all right? I was asking myself, alone in this silly wooden cabin, weeping. Even Cindy had a kind moment: she curled up at the foot of my bed. Meg—any way I can be of help, please let me know. Do you want to come out West and stay with me? Do you need money? Should I come there?

Later—

You know, Meg sister, I don't drink alcohol anymore. But I'm feeling drunk. Piano tinklings from Ancer Peak's up the road. I wish it were traffic noise or sirens.

Today I was walking through the town, back from getting my mail. I'd been hoping for a card from George—all this time and I still haven't heard from him. And I passed the back of the school playground; it is a tiny plot of cement, attached to a rather weathered brick Methodist church school. These children will be in school in another week or so, but now they are here to play free, their last bit of summer. I could not see the children, but I heard them. Wild laughing shrieks; high-pitched, delighted singing. Names called out. Once in a while, a mother's voice, but it was soft, not mean, not critical. Breathless children, overcome with joy.

Meg, was I ever a child like that? Did I ever run madly in circles until I was dizzy and laughing, and then fall hard on my butt? Do you have any memory of me climbing to the top of the playground slide and throwing out my arms? Was I exhilarated and proud and heedless as I pushed myself down the long, dangerous scoop of silver to land on my knees in the sand?

I think I missed all that, Meg. Perhaps some expensive therapy will explain it all to me. Today, as I walked passed the schoolyard, children's laughter was like African folk songs—beautiful, but from an exotic elsewhere, unknown to me, apart from my experience. What I do wonder though is, If I was not jumping and running and singing as a child—what was I doing?

Do you remember—you were maybe eight and I was four—when the maid broke that antique gravy boat? It was irreplaceable and part of a set. Mother was furious. She knocked over a lamp, I think, and called the maid names. Everyone watched this display, watched it spiral down with her exhaustion. Then Mother simply emitted one of her quiet, falsely forgiving sighs. "Well, nothing is forever," she said, and patted the distraught maid's shoulder.

I remember that she slapped you a lot in your early teen years and that you never cried. She would cry. What were those slaps for, what disagreements, what broken rules? I remember she did not like your clothes and was mad about your hair, too. You learned to come and go, come and go—off to schools, away on trips, not looking back at any of us from airplane windows.

By my adolescence you were gone. I learned to make no demands at home, to remain unnervingly polite, but detached. I was sleeping with my math teacher, you know, when I was sixteen, but no one ever found out—it was the tidiest mess imaginable. Mr. Ackerman. I broke it off with him and he gave me a B+. And I never crashed a car, never had beer on my breath, always got good marks.

I do not think Mother enjoyed her family; only that she accepted it, tolerated it, and, finally, acted as though she cherished it. The years went on, and her tantrums ceased. When we were little, she was mad; later on, she was sad. And disconnected somehow from us, as though we did not really come from her and she had not made our lives. If you notice, she will never volunteer memories of our childhood, of the houses we lived in, the trips we took. I don't think she has any fondness for the past.

You were saying, the last time I saw you, that you wanted to make sure you were not the kind of mother to Audrey that our mother was to us. Which I've reflected on quite a bit since. Our mother was remote, troubled, easily offended, uninterested in our childhood concerns. It was as though we were interrupting her life, rather than enhancing it. Are these qualities ones you can avoid with your little girl? Because, I think, knowing Mother better now, that really she was just terrified of her children. Who knows why? Terrified of the responsibility, of the ways we might reflect her, of the requirement that she attend to these powerless beings in ways, perhaps, she did not feel she could. Maybe she was terrified of being like her own mother. . . .

Meg—

You may be wondering why I'm still here. I was planning to leave at the end of last week. I'd even done most of my packing. And then, one late night, after I'd been up reading for several hours, I decided to take Cindy for a walk, just to feel some air. She was willing, but hardly eager, and both of us trudged along sleepily. There was a pleasant breeze from the ocean and Ancer Peak's piano was playing some melancholy Gershwin songs—quite beautiful, seeming to blend with the natural sounds of the trees and water around me.

At the end of the road, of course, Cindy stopped short. We were too near Jane's house, a place Cindy will not go near or even look at. But I looked, as I have a few other times.

Then, I saw Jane. She passed by the window briefly, dragging on a cigarette. Had I not actually seen her, I would have turned in a second and gone back home; but I wanted to see her again. Had I not seen her, maybe I would be back in San Francisco now.

There she was, passing across the square of lighted window, pausing for one beat, then moving on. She was pacing. I crouched low, held my hand on Cindy's indignant neck.

Jane continued pacing, and she was moving her arms, her head was bobbing up and down. She was clearly in some kind of conversation. Then a compulsion struck me—and, Meg, I'm not proud of this, just reporting it to you. I wanted to hear what she was saying. This square window was the frame of a photograph; Jane, with her uncombed long hair, her angry face, her baggy clothing, was the image. But the image was not enough for me. I needed to listen.

I tugged a bit at Cindy's leash, but she would not follow me. "All right, stay here. Stay, Cindy. I'll come back in one minute, you just stay."

I walked down the road a little ways and then crossed a plot of brown, overgrown grass and weeds, part of Jane's property, and stood next to a plum tree in her yard. I was maybe twenty feet from her kitchen window. Beneath it was a pile of rotting stuff: melon rinds covered with ashes, empty soup cans, and some paper cups with faces drawn on them.

At first, I could hear Jane's voice but not her words, and I was disappointed. I considered moving closer, just under the window, where an old rusted barrel was leaning. But then she was speaking louder, clearer.

"You never say anything, Russell. Why don't you ever say what you're thinking." Pacing, smoking. "I know you're thinking things, but you never say them. Why is that?"

"I don't know," came a tiny voice. The little boy, I supposed. I raised up on my toes and could see the messy hair on the back of his head, which pivoted with his mother's movements, like someone watching a ping-pong game.

"*People have to speak up their minds, Russell. That's how you get anywhere in the world.*" Jane stood still then. I saw her stub out her cigarette. She was facing her son, so she was facing the window. She was looking at the boy, but I was truly panicked for some seconds that she was really looking at me, could see or sense me.

"*Two kinds of people in the world, Russell. The kind that speaks their mind and the kind that's afraid to. You're not ever going to get any better, Russell. Not unless you start telling me what's on your mind.*"

This too, sent eerie shivers through me, as though the words were meant for me, rather than for Russell. And what did she mean, anyway? Better, how? And what could be on the mind of a six-year-old?

When Jane turned away to pour herself some coffee, I stealthily scooted out of her yard, back to Cindy, who I could swear looked at me with disapproval. I grabbed her leash and wound it around my hand and we started back to George's; but I looked back once more. Now I could not listen; the scene was a photograph again. Jane, standing above her son, her arms folded in front of her, her head tilted to the right in a scolding, berating attitude. Had the boy been bad? Would he be punished?

7

Jane's kitchen was dark. The sun was just setting. She had been sitting at the table for some time, smoking and slapping cards down in a distracted game of solitaire. Her pens and papers were beside her, for earlier she had been figuring her accounts. The pillowcases hung as curtains over the window had not been cleaned or aired in many months. She peered through where they separated, and she could see Russell, sitting on the tire swing, kicking his bare foot in the grass beneath him. He was wearing one of the masks Jane had made for him; this was a pig's snout, held over his nose by a string around his head. In the morning, Russell had gotten into the candy again and Jane was almost breathless with fury. And this was his punishment. "If you act like a little pig, you're going to be one," she hissed at him. As she angrily muttered that he had to learn his lesson, that this was all for his own good, Jane fixed the mask over his face and pushed him out the back door.

Spots on her temples ached mercilessly and sent pain through her head, down to her neck. She lit another cigarette from the butt end of her last. She kept her eye on Russell, who looked so sad, so confused.

No sweets at all when Jane was a little girl. Mama did not approve of sweets. No cards either, or dancing, or talking to boys. These were rules enforced not by threats and raised voices, but by her mother's tears. The sisters were so placating, accommodating, so bullied by the weepy scenes. Jane felt disgusted, then contemptuous. Her mother was weak, and Jane felt compelled to protest and challenge. She remembered her girlhood as one long dispute: Mother's pathetic grievances, the cowardly mediating of Ellen and Jesse and Lucille, and her own defiant rebel yells.

Jane didn't like to see her little boy sad. But she had to be firm. There were no sweets at all when she was a little girl.

The neighbor's piano was being tuned; the sound carried and worsened Jane's headache. "I'd like to murder that little faggot one of these days," she said, stubbing out her cigarette.

Where was Dr. Landau? Jane had left a message, but the doctor had not returned the call. Thinks I'm crazy, Jane reflected bitterly. Thinks I'm making it all up, or imagining it all. What right does she have to judge me? I know my boy, I know my boy better than she does. A Jew with no kids of her own; what does she know? What would it take for that cunt to believe me anyway? Does Russell have to drop dead?

Jane called out: "Russell!" She did not lean out the window or go to the door; she merely lifted her head and howled out the boy's name, and the sound echoed in the small, dark kitchen, like a cry of pain. Russell appeared at the door. Jane would not look at him. The piano tuning stopped, then began again.

"That's enough punishment, I guess. Come on inside."

Russell softly pushed the screen door and slid into the room. He removed the mask from his face and placed it on the table.

Jane looked at him then. She presented a broad smile, but it was disingenuous: it was a contrast to her cold, angry eyes. "I have a treat for you now," she told him. "Sit here." The boy hopped onto the wooden chair, not yet cheered, not yet forgetting his humiliating punishment.

Jane rose and left the kitchen and when she returned she had a large tin box with a red cross on its cover.

"Medicine? That's the medicine box," Russell said.

"Yes, but there's something special in here. I keep it in here, just for you." She lifted the cover and removed a square of aluminum foil.

"That's candy?" the boy asked, astonished.

"Yes, it's special candy that will help you get better, Russell." What Jane unwrapped was an over-the-counter laxative preparation which looked like a chocolate bar, divided into squares. She broke off a piece and gave it to the boy.

Unhesitatingly, Russell popped it in his mouth. "Tastes funny," he said, and made a displeased face.

Jane explained that this was different from other candy. Other candy was bad for little boys, but this was good for them. And he must eat the whole bar. And he must have another bar two hours from now. Russell said: "No, no, I don't like this."

She bent down, put her face close to his. "You're going to eat this, Russell. You're going to eat this whole bar of chocolate."

The boy was ill late into the night. He vomited, first, and then of course was plagued with diarrhea, cramps. Jane remained calm. She patted his forehead and cheeks with a cool, damp cloth. She gave him sips of water and pieces of the laxative candy; she would hurry him to the bathroom and stand above him as his bowels moved uncontrollably, with a violent noise. The little boy said nothing during this ordeal. He was shaking, breathing shallowly, his face was red. He cried very softly. But he did not question Jane or even look at her.

Jane kept her arms crossed over her chest. "It's all right, Russell. This is supposed to happen. Don't worry." The walls of the tiny bathroom were covered with faded, stained wallpaper; the pattern had gulls soaring. The odor in the room was sweet, not offensive, and reminded Jane of when Russell was a baby.

She helped him back to bed, fastened the belts over him. She sat in the rocking chair that had been hers since she was a little girl. She watched him drift into and out of sleep. Just before daylight, some birds rested on the tree outside Russell's room, and they were singing.

"Jane, am I very sick, Jane?"

"Yes, Russell," she said, resentfully. "And I'm going to call that goddamn Landau back tomorrow."

Some moments passed. The birds sang. Morning's silver light was just filtering into the tiny sickroom. In a voice too weak even to reveal his fear and misery, Russell asked: "Read to me?"

8

Dear Meg—

Not much new, really. Cindy started wheezing and coughing. I was not so much worried as irritated. I took her to the veterinary clinic some miles out of town. I consistently find vets to be kind, inoffensive people, if not terribly profound. Anyway, in the pleasant waiting room, decorated with paintings of cats and dogs and posters about loving your pet, a large woman swung open the door and stomped in. She was carrying a cat cage and set it down roughly. She was extremely belligerent with the soft-spoken young woman behind the desk.

Big woman: "Bootie still has that ear infection. I was just here two days ago."

Receptionist: "Yes, I remember Bootie. Have you been using the drops the doctor prescribed?"

Big woman, bellowing: "Of course I have! And cleaning with a Q-tip. And the thing's oozing even more blood and pus than it was before."

Receptionist, remarkably composed: "Well, have a seat, madam, and the doctor can take a look."

Big woman: "I paid eighty-three dollars my last visit here. And the problem's just gotten worse."

Receptionist, patiently, gesturing toward a chair: "I understand."

"I want this cat cured. Once and for all!"

This miserable woman actually slid the cat cage across the floor in one kick with her foot. Then she seated herself next to me. I had the strongest impulse to tell her that maybe her cat was going to die; that we all had to die sometime; that nothing lasts forever. But I kept quiet.

Turns out Cindy's got hairballs and will be fine. She liked riding in the car. But she did not look out the window; she kept her eyes on me. Maybe we're becoming friends.

Later—

Loneliness, now. Not a feeling; it's a thing. It is solid, undeniable. It hits me. I want to go home. Why don't I go home?

I remember you, racing and recklessly pushing through the wash on the line— brilliant white flapping sheets—and howling like a warrior. Then you're stopped in your tracks. A shadow has loomed. Of Mother.

(Is it a cruel fashion, some kind of misguided agenda of our times, which blames the mother? For what? For codifying our natural responses and creating unfathomable goals? For insisting we aspire? Like religion, the mother implicitly understands that her child are imperfect, incapable, prone to straying. Bad. And we need her; we need to be stopped in our tracks, to be shown the right way. That is the old-fashioned Mother-God, which shifted in this century to a seemingly more satisfying, but surely as superstitious image: Mother-Neurotic. The agonizing revelation of these modern days is that Mother is human; that her wisdom and guidance are inextricably bound to her needs, to what she has repressed, to her fears and beliefs. To her mother. Which reveals that she is not God. Only a person. And the shattering of that myth is traumatic, infuriating, somehow unacceptable. If she is not perfect, then what is? So Mother becomes a sort of grand fall guy in a way that an image of God never could. She is the origin of life, participating in our innocence, knowing us, mirroring us; she is also the source of pain, constraint, deviance, alienation, sorrow.

When we are mourning the loss of our first days in the sun—which we inevitably will—somehow, simply because she was present for those days, the loss is her fault. Couldn't she have warned us that life would sting so much? After our nightmares instead of banal comforting and dismissal, couldn't she have told the truth: that life would be full of bad dreams, descending arbitrarily. Not a damn thing you can do about it, kid. The mother is blamed for preparing us for a merciful world that does not exist.)

Because it was not Mother's shadow that inhibited you. That was, and still is, a comfortable assumption. I remember that day, Meg. It was the shadow of some gigantic bird, swooping down too close over our heads. You called to me: "Run, Paul, run away," and I did, and hid under the wooden porch steps, where I stared with huge,

*unblinking, terrified eyes. Then you crawled in beside me. "It's fine now," you assured
me. "That bird has flown away."*

You saved me.

(That's how I remember it.)

Thank you, Meg.

PART III

I

Jane swerved her Pontiac into the gravel parking lot of the T & T Cocktail Lounge. She shut off the headlights, slid out of the car, slammed the door hard. She walked fast under yellow floodlights to the open door of the bar. She had no coat, no pocketbook. She wore loose-fitting trousers and a heavy plaid shirt; her hair hung limp, uncombed, down her back.

The barman knew her and nodded, but the two did not speak. He was a large, dark man with hairy arms. He wiped his hands lazily on a cloth which hung from his belt and poured Jane a glass of water and a shot glass of scotch. She downed her liquor, chased it with a small swallow, and then lifted her chin at the barman, to indicate she'd take another. She sat on a stool at the bar. She swung herself around, and leaned back, resting her elbows on the bar counter behind her.

Against one wall was a jukebox, and there were a few tables in the place. In the center of the room a square of floor was bordered by blinking red Christmas lights, and a rotating mirror ball hung above; this space was for dancing, but no one danced at the T & T, and the sparkling lights were just sad, like a crumpled party invitation or deflated balloons.

The heat from Russell's forehead still burned Jane's palm. She could not think of Russell now. A picture of Russell as she'd left him thirty minutes before assaulted her: skin pink and wet from a fever, lips pale, eyes half-closed. She'd made him sit up straight and sip some cola. He had been too weak, had slid back down against his pillows and Jane yelled at him: "Fine, then, don't drink anything, and you'll dry up!" His eyes were neither fully open nor fully closed. "Sleep, goddamn you," she whispered, and finally she fastened the ties over him in bed and left the house furious at the boy.

Two women sat down the bar from Jane, leaning toward each other, talking rapidly but quietly. One of the women was absently stirring her cocktail with her finger.

In a corner a young man was sitting alone at a table. He was holding a cigarette, rolling its unlighted end against the edge of a glass ashtray. He wore a dark-green shirt and dark-green pants—some kind of uniform, Jane was thinking; but there were no soldiers around here anymore. His trouser cuffs were rolled up, exposing his ankles. In this light, the man's skin was copper-colored, his hair was shiny black. His eyes were gray.

He sat perfectly still, his legs spread apart. He stared ahead of him as though in a trance, as though he were not at a table in the T & T at all, but might have been anywhere: in a café in Paris, on a subway train, at a funeral or a wedding, in a jail cell.

Jane knew this man. She knew him. Somehow, his qualities, his personality were evident to Jane. She swallowed her second drink and called for a third.

A soldier? A cowboy? A killer? He was restless. He was an angry and impatient man. Jane knew him. He stayed at a motel down the highway, Jane reckoned, and he kept the heavy drapes closed. At night, he fell to sleep long after midnight with the severe ceiling light still on, dressed only in pants and socks, with a magazine open and a bottle of flat beer on the floor beside his bed. This man could not drift cozily, languorously to sleep; he could only pass out, his consciousness wandering not off to a dream, but away from what's real. Pass out frowning, with the beer taste in his mouth, calmed in dreamless sleep by the sound of trucks passing on the highway. And in the morning, he'd sit up straight, look around his room, alert and fearful, take a deep breath—oh, yes, he'd recall, here I am, here I am. Through the day, his black brow was tight, his gray eyes distant. Lonely. Empty.

"Don't I know you?" Jane stood above him, holding her glass.

"No," said the young man, keeping his head motionless but rolling his eyes upward to see her.

Jane pulled a chair over with her foot and straddled it, her arms folded over its back. "I'd swear I know you," she said, smiling as though to insult him.

"Haven't been in this town long enough to know people," the man replied.

"I don't mean know you that way. I don't mean that we've met and talked. I mean I *know* you."

"Maybe you're saying you know my type?"

Jane slapped her hand on the table. "That's it. That's right. That's just what I mean. I know your type, soldier. Very well."

The barman coughed, then turned away, and the two women who'd been whispering stayed quiet to hear this interaction between Jane and the stranger.

"Usually," said the young man, "when people feel they know you, it's because they think they're just like you. They don't really know you; they just know themselves. Do you think we're alike—you and me? I mean, can people really be all that alike?"

Jane rested her chin on her fist now. "That's a strange question. That's a profound question. It's the kind of thing I talk about with Russell a lot: Different kinds of people in the world, and how they get that way, and how they meet up, and why. It's one of the puzzles of life, isn't it?"

The stranger tipped his bottle and swallowed the last of his beer; Jane watched his strong, handsome throat. "Well," he said, "tell me how you think we're alike."

Jane whispered: "I'll tell you some other time. I won't tell you now when these crazies are listening in." She jerked her head in the direction of the bar and the other patrons. "They just love to jeer at me."

The man laughed. "Okay, okay. And who's this Russell? A boyfriend?"

"Russell's her little boy," the barman called out as he wiped a mug and stacked it with the others. "Cutest little boy."

Jane swung her head quickly to face him. "No one's asking *you* anything. No one's asking you if my boy's cute or not cute." Then she turned back to the stranger. "Russell's real sick. Has been sick all his life."

The man shifted in his seat now for the first time, sat straighter. "Sick? What's he sick with?"

Jane did not hear, but one of the women at the bar whispered: "Sick with Jane, that's what," and the other woman giggled.

"It's a long, sad story," Jane told the man. "It's very sad. I can tell you about it if you want. But not here. I couldn't talk about it in here."

"Is it cancer?" the man asked, and those eyes Jane thought she knew were gazing at her sincerely, directly. Jane shook her head. "Is it a mental problem? Or something wrong with his organs?"

"They don't know," said Jane, loudly, desperately. She held her palm to her forehead. "They can't figure out what's wrong with Russell. I've had him to all the best doctors, and they can't figure out what's wrong."

The barman murmured, contemptuously: "Best doctors. Can't figure out what's wrong."

"I *hear* you," Jane shouted and rose, and stood in the center of the bar staring at the big man behind the counter. "I hear your snide comments. You don't know what I've been through." Her voice was a single pitch, of defense and accusation, like that of one school bully standing up to another. "People around here think they . . . people around here think they . . ."

The barman was frowning; the women sat straight, their mouths slightly open. Facing the barman, Jane held up her arms, curled at the elbow; her hands formed tiny firm fists; her feet were planted apart in an old-fashioned fighter's pose. "I'll take you people on if I have to!" Jane screamed, closing her eyes. "I'll take any of you people on!"

No one moved then. Someone said: "Drunk." Someone else said: "Jane's insane." These mean words had no effect on Jane; she kept her stance, prepared to do battle.

The stranger rose quietly and stepped behind Jane. "Now, no need for all of this. Let's go on outside for some air. Let's have a talk."

"Wait a minute, then, wait just one minute, cowboy," Jane said, and quickly walked across the long, dark floor to the ladies' room. Inside, she leaned over the sink to look at her face in the mirror. She moistened her pale lips with her tongue. She smiled. Jane's teeth were all a brown-yellow. "I shouldn't smile," she whispered, "because these teeth are so ugly."

She took a step back. She delicately glided two fingers through her hair, because it seemed so lifeless. She looked at herself in the mirror, turning to one side, then the other. Jane winked.

2

"No. No, I don't go for that stuff," Jane told the man. She flicked her cigarette onto the gravel of the parking lot. They were sitting on the muddy fender of Jane's car. There was a half-moon this night, and the lights from the T & T cast a smoky, golden glow and shadows over them.

"It isn't what you think," he said, in a gentle voice, looking at her.

"I've been around that stuff, soldier. I know all about it." She folded her arms over her chest, looked away from him. A small breeze blew Jane's hair across her forehead. "My mother and my sisters used to talk about all of that. My mother had a church she went to. She prayed a lot. And when I was a little girl, the traveling preachers would come here, to this town. Selling their Bibles. Selling little bottles of potions—or, I don't know what it was. The Witnesses, they called themselves."

The man seemed exhausted; he closed his eyes, leaned back his head, rolled it each way.

"You have a stiff neck, cowboy-soldier?"

The man looked at Jane now. "You misunderstand me, Jane. It's a different kind of religion I believe in. I'm not talking about preachers and churches. I'm talking about you and your little boy."

"I won't pray for Russell, if that's what you mean. I don't believe in that stuff. That superstitious stuff."

"I'm talking about you, your little boy, that ocean out there, that highway out there. The sky, the forest. Your sisters."

"My sisters? My sisters and the sky and the forest?" Jane slid off the car fender and took a few steps across the gravel, turned in a reckless circle, stuck her hands firmly in her trousers pockets. "Well, I guess I don't know *what* you're talking about. Do *you* know what you're talking about?" and Jane began to laugh.

The man lowered his head; he laced his fingers together. He looked like a small child, then, his black hair blown by the wind.

"Oh, hey, I'm sorry," said Jane, but she was still laughing. "Listen, I'm sorry. Listen, why don't I go in and get us a couple of beers? How would that be?"

The man, not looking at Jane, spoke softly, deliberately, as though recalling lines of a poem: "Things aren't what they seem. They're more than what they seem. But, at the same time, less. You said you knew me, Jane, but you don't know me."

"Oh, yes."

"No." The stranger shook his head, as though mightily disappointed, discouraged. He said: "A baby can be in his cradle and a thief can come in the room. The thief is looking to steal some money. But the baby will not know the thief."

"Because the baby's too little to know what a thief is. Of course."

"Because—no, Jane. The baby cannot recognize a thief, because he does not yet have a thief in him. A genius can hold the baby, but the baby will not recognize a genius. A liar can coo at the baby, but the baby won't see a liar. A saint can look into the baby's eyes, but the baby won't know the saint."

"What is all this? Something about babies being pure?"

"I'm saying, I'm trying to say—you can only know what's in you."

Jane ran inside the T & T and ordered two bottles of beer, and as she was putting down the bills to pay, the barman said: "You know that fellow?"

"Know him? Yes, I know him."

"You know he was in a mental hospital then, don't you?"

"I know that," Jane said, without blinking.

"You know he's not all right in his mind?"

She took the beer bottles. "I know you're not all right in your mind." And after the screen door had tapped closed behind her, she called into the T & T, to the barman and the ladies at the bar: "None of us is all right in our minds, are we?"

The man was standing now, smoking a cigarette, leaning against Jane's car, scraping the toe of his boot in the gravel. He continued: "Your sisters and the sky and the forest and you and your little boy. Sickness, war. Flowers. Us, right here, tonight. Sad memories and happy memories."

"Yes?" Jane asked impatiently.

"Everything. I'm talking about everything. Life."

"Life. Well, what exactly is your religion, then?"

"That's it. Life."

"Life. Well, that's a good one," she murmured sarcastically. "That's a religion we all have to practice whether we believe in it or not."

The man looked up at Jane and smiled. "The religious people call it God. Miracles and grace. And God's will. Faith. But the word, the real word is Life." He was looking directly into her eyes, his voice restrained, telling a soft, gentle story; and yet his gaze and the way he held himself were intense, unpredictable. "God is in all life. And we are life. God is in all things. God is present in all light, every wind."

"God's in this bottle of beer," said Jane, mocking him, "and I'll drink to that." She lifted the bottle to her lips and gulped heartily.

But the stranger was not deterred. "God's in our veins. God's in prisons and houses and trucks and airplanes. God's in the sand, the grass, the moon. In the colors in a painting. Jazz music. Dope fiends."

"God is everywhere, sees everything. Am I right?"

"No, no, I don't know. I don't know what God *does.* Whether God sees or thinks or feels. I only know what it is. It is life."

"It's all the same corny stuff, soldier. I've heard them talk about it as far back as I can remember. If God is in everything, why do so many bad things happen?"

"But why *shouldn't* they happen?" the man answered.

"Oh, you're saying there's a reason for everything?"

The man sighed deeply; for the first time he seemed frustrated. "I don't know if there's a reason for everything, Jane. And if there is, I couldn't give the reason. I don't understand any more than what I've told you. That everything is God. That life is God. *Your* life."

Jane had become distracted, though, with her own resentments. "And everyone's a hypocrite. Everyone talks God, but then they cheat and lie and steal. They don't love each other, or give, or pray. They just go around telling everyone else how to live. Everyone's always been telling me how to live. And then when people are in trouble—getting their divorces or on their deathbeds—then they pray."

"Your life is your God. My life is my God. All life is all our God. You see?"

Jane turned away from him now, and spoke fiercely. "No, I *don't* see. I don't like people trying to force their beliefs on me. I don't want any religious stuff. I don't want it from a preacher on a corner or a priest in the church or you"—now she faced him—"or you, sitting on my car, drunk and sexy and straight from a nuthouse."

"I love you" was the man's answer, toneless, barely audible.

But these words only further angered Jane. "I'm not stupid, cowboy. I may be the monster everyone says I am. But I'm not stupid."

"I love you."

She walked quickly to him and leaned against him and put her lips to his ear. "Fuck me then? Fuck me right here, right here in this parking lot?"

"I love you," he repeated.

"Then will you give me some money?"

"I love you."

"*Stop* saying that," Jane cried and she threw her half-finished bottle far out toward the highway. They heard it whisk through the summer air and crash onto pavement and shatter.

3

"Where are you from, soldier?" They were sitting now on the hood of Jane's car. They were smoking cigarettes. One of the car doors was open, a butterscotch light from the dashboard shone, and the radio was playing big band tunes softly.

"California. South of here. And then I've traveled a lot."

"What about your family?"

"My parents died."

"Do you miss them?"

"No. I don't miss anyone. I don't miss any time or place or people."

"I miss my sisters. But I hate them, too. And sometimes I miss my mother. Sometimes when I'm sitting with Russell and reading to him, I will miss my mother."

"Where is your little boy now?"

"Home in bed. He had a fever earlier."

"You love him very much?"

Jane did not answer.

"I think," said the stranger, "that you do love him very much but that you're afraid maybe you don't."

"I'm afraid I don't—what? Love Russell?"

"Yes, you're afraid you don't love him. Could that be true?"

"That's a pretty terrible thing to say, soldier."

"Do you touch the boy?"

"What do you mean? What do you mean, do I touch him?"

"Rock him, hold him, hug him, caress him?" The man moved closer to Jane; their faces were only inches away, as in confrontation.

"Are you mad at me?" Jane whispered.

The man whispered, too, even more softly, so that Jane could barely hear him. "No. I love you. I want to help you."

Jane closed her eyes. "I can't touch Russell. I used to. I don't anymore."

"Well, you *can* touch him, you know. I can help you touch Russell. Take me with you. Let's go to Russell."

"He's sick. I think he's going to die." The air had become suddenly still. Jane's face was flushed. She kept her lips tight, her eyes open wide.

"Let's go," the man offered. He took Jane by the arm.

The barman and his customers stood at the big dusty window of the T & T, behind a neon beer sign. They watched Jane and the stranger climb into Jane's car. They were shocked about Jane, and they were frightened for her. They shook their heads as the car eased out of the parking lot and onto the highway, and after they had watched its red lights disappear around a bend, they turned away, in silence.

4

"How did you come to know all these things?" Jane asked her new friend as she drove toward home. She had been crying.

"I was in a hospital room," said the man. He watched the road ahead of him as he spoke. His window was open and his hair was blown wildly about. "I was alone in a room and they wouldn't let me out. There was wire over the window and a lock on the door. They brought me food. They were kind to me. They smiled at me. I think they liked me very much. And so I was in this room all day and all night. I had nothing to do."

"You didn't have any books or newspapers?"

"No. I don't think so. I don't remember books or newspapers."

"Did you get to be with the other patients? They must have let you be with the other patients," Jane wondered.

"Sometimes. Yes, sometimes I played cards with a group of men. But mostly I was alone, in the bare room. With nothing to do but think. And then the strangest thing happened to me, Jane. I got tired of thinking. All of a sudden, I didn't want any more thoughts."

Jane found herself pushing her foot harder on the gas pedal; the car sped faster along the winding, narrow highway.

The man lit a cigarette. "So, I tried to stop thinking, you know, I tried to empty my head of all thoughts. And it didn't work at first. It didn't work for a long time. Because a question would pop into my brain"—the stranger laughed now, recalling his struggle—"or I would hear a sound or notice a bug crawling, and that would get me to thinking. Which is just what I didn't want. Thinking."

"Well, what did you want?"

The man did not reply for some seconds. "Just to be," he said finally. "Just to be, and that's how I found God."

"It's quite a philosophy," Jane said, suddenly resentful. She slowed the Pontiac, turned the wheel, and pulled up onto a grassy patch near her porch. "Quite a philosophy," she repeated, more tenderly, subdued. "Why should I believe the things you say?"

"I am not asking you to believe anything. Not at all," the man said, shrugging his shoulders. "But, you do believe the things I say. Don't you?"

"Yes."

"Completely? With all your heart?"

"I think Russell is sick," said Jane, and she had said it many times now to the stranger, but now her tone and expression were utterly defeated. "I think he's dying, and no one believes me."

"It doesn't matter."

"It doesn't matter? That Russell is sick? Or that no one believes me?"

"Neither thing matters. Nothing matters, really."

"That's so sad, that's so . . ."

The man smiled generously and gasped, caught his breath, placed his hand with fingers spread apart against his chest. "You think I'm sad, Jane? See, you really don't know me."

"And why should I trust you? The things you say, the things you claim to know?"

"Well, that's it. I don't know why. You just do."

5

The stranger had said he would not come back. The stranger said he'd stay with Jane, and with Russell, and show Jane how she could love the boy, but then he would leave and not return. Jane made them tea and they sat for some hours in the dimly lit kitchen, smoking and talking.

"I'm tired," she told him, and he said nothing. "I realize all of a sudden, you know, how tired I am. Of being so angry and hungry, and of fighting, fighting fighting—" Here her voice rose, with remembrance of the sisters and the mother and the stares of neighbors as she walked through her cold, dirty town. "Fighting."

"You're tired of your delusion, Jane."

"My demon?"

"No, no, no. No demon. *Delusion.*"

She looked at him and blinked and moisture filled her eyes as a question. "What is my delusion?"

"You know."

"No. No. I don't know, you tell me, what is my delusion?"

"That you are you."

Just then, Jane was flustered and upset her cup of lukewarm tea, and the copper-colored liquid formed a puddle, dripped onto the black-and-white checked tile floor. "Shit, shit," Jane said, reacting. The man only smiled.

The man put his palms to his cheeks and then pushed his hands through his hair. "Yes, you're deluded into thinking that you are you. That you have some feelings, some thoughts, some memories. That your boy is sick and your life is lonely. That you suffer."

"The Bible says—"

"I don't read the Bible—"

" 'Blessed are the poor in spirit: for theirs is the kingdom of heaven.' "

"Can't read, really. Just a little bit."

She reached to him suddenly, put her hand over his cold knuckles. "I am the poor in spirit, soldier. I am, I really am."

"That's your delusion."

"Then who am I? If I'm not really me"—and she was frowning now, speaking harshly—"*who am I?*"

The man said he could not tell Jane that. But he would teach her something: how to touch her son.

Later, Jane sat by the lighted fire, with her legs curled under her in a dilapidated armchair; its stuffing was coming out at the corners, and Jane absently fiddled with the torn upholstery. At the top of the stairs, the stranger appeared, carrying her son, asleep, in his arms. The stranger was so handsome then. His shirt was unbuttoned and Jane wanted to feel his brown chest. He proceeded down the short staircase, carrying the boy, and Jane watched the man's strong muscles, of his thighs, of his arms and shoulders.

"Here is Russell," the man said, standing before Jane. He laid the boy across her lap, and the boy's body was light and limp, like a doll.

Jane held her hands up against her cheeks, the palms flat, fearfully, as though her son were some animal whose reactions could not be predicted.

The man kneeled down beside the chair. "He's a sick boy, Jane?"

"He can't hear," she declared. "He can't hear but they can't figure out why he can't hear. Now I think, too, that he's losing the power to speak. That's what I think is happening. He's getting thinner and weaker, too. He's had abcesses in his mouth. He gets rashes on his scalp. Russell is . . . wasting away."

The man took Jane's left hand. He put his own hand flat against hers.

"But the doctors don't believe me," she said.

He closed his eyes, leaned back his head. "No," he said. "No, not this hand I don't think. Give me your other hand."

"No," said Jane, emphatically. "I'm scared."

The stranger was stern. "Give me the hand. I need to hold your other hand."

She acquiesced. She could see that she was surrendering to the man's orders, maybe even to his ideas, and her rebellions were momentary, not deeply felt. "Are you trying to get me saved?" she wanted to know.

"Saved from what?"

"From sinning, I guess. From all that stuff they want you to get saved from."

"People," said the stranger, looking at Jane's face, then at her neck, then at her breasts. "People are either unsavable, or they're already free. You're already free."

"How can I be *free* when my *little boy* is suffering?"

"Trust me."

"Tell me again—why should I believe you, the things you say, the things you want?" she asked, but less as a challenge now.

"Because I'm happy, Jane. Doesn't that mean something to you?"

("Happiness is everything," Jane's mother said when she was dying. "That's why you come to the Lord. So you can die happy. You can be saved, and know you're going to be taken care of, and be happy." And Jane had bawled at her mother: "That's a stupid story, that's a stupid story you're just telling yourself to make yourself feel better." "To be happy, Jane. Don't *you* want to be happy?" "No," Jane had said.)

"Sometimes," Jane said, "sometimes it seems that what comes out of my mouth is not really what I really believe." She looked down, spoke softly, as though she were confessing a long-held, shameful secret.

The stranger nodded, closed his eyes for a moment.

"I mean that what I say and how I act are not really me. I am not who I think I am."

The man held her right hand now. He pressed it between both of his hands. "Warmth," he whispered. "Now, do like this—" And he illustrated rubbing the tips of the fingers and the thumb together in a circular motion. "Does it feel hot?" he asked.

"A little warm," Jane answered.

"Not hot?"

"No." She continued the rubbing. "Well . . ." Jane said, tilting her head to one side. "Well . . . yes. Now. It is hot. It is."

"It should get very hot, Jane."

"It is. Very hot. Oh!" And she was startled, as though her fingertips had actually been burned.

"Right," said the stranger, sounding cold and competent. He rose and stood back a few steps. "Right. Now, put that hand flat but gentle on the top of Russell's head. Press his head, firmly."

Jane did as she was told.

"What are you thinking about now, Jane?"

"I don't know," she said, urgently. "Should I be thinking of something? Should I be—?"

"No, no, don't worry about that now. Press his head. Now take that hand and put it over his ear. First one ear, then the other ear."

Jane complied with the instructions.

"Now, take the hand and hold it against his throat. Just hold it there, softly, not pressing. Feel his breathing, feel how he swallows in his sleep."

By this time, the man had seated himself, cross-legged, on the other side of the room, in a shadow. He watched as Jane repeated these motions, touching her sleeping child. "Close your eyes, Jane. Do you see light?"

"Light?"

"When your eyes are closed, is it light?"

"Yes," answered Jane, astonished.

"And what do you hear?"

"Something . . . like wind. Wind? Soft wind."

"When your eyes are closed, when you're touching Russell, you see light and hear wind?"

"Yes," she called out, as though the man had gone away. "Yes, and I hear your voice."

The man said: "If, when your eyes are closed, everything is God— then, when your eyes are open, everything will be God."

They were silent for some time; the man stayed across the room, out of the light. Jane was most absorbed in the body stretched out across her lap, the head of her little boy leaning against her breast. "Am I healing him?" she said.

An hour passed, and another. She held Russell still and close, but gently, stroked his cheeks with her warm hand. She could not see the man. Into the darkness and clutter of their house she said: "Russell is being healed, I'm healing him."

"Hello?" she whispered. Had the man gone?

Russell opened his eyes, then. He looked around, surprised to be in his mother's arms, to be out of his bed. He smiled.

"How do you feel, Russell?" Jane asked the boy, in a more tender and inviting way than she was used to asking things of him.

Russell answered as he answered most questions: "I don't know."

She placed her right hand on his forehead. She pressed in the way the stranger had told her. Jane smiled. "You're cured now, Russell. There's been a miracle and you're cured."

The boy sat up and slid from his mother's lap. "A miracle? A really truly miracle?"

"Yes, Russell."

He went to her, thrust his body between her legs, put his tiny hands on her knees. "You are looking like you're happy, Jane. Are you happy?"

Jane was exhausted. Tears welled in her cold eyes, then fell over her hard, pale cheeks. She opened her arms, and Russell fell into her embrace.

6

Dear Meg:

I've sent this to you care of Mother, because she said you and Audrey would be staying with her for several weeks. Good idea, I think. I feel I have little to offer you, by way of advice (although I'm sure Mother is handling that just fine). Only my support and love. And a promise not to lecture you on a) the inherent stupidities and oppressiveness of marriage and of heterosexual life or b) what a jerk I always thought Bert was.

Just this morning, I heard a woman from the town, named Fern Welch, telling her mother, Constance Welch, that Jane had gone into the school last week to register her little son for the semester and had had a fight with the principal. "And she stormed out of that place," said Welch the younger, "screaming that she wouldn't let her son go to that school no matter what." "Screaming?" asked the astonished Welch mother. "That's right. And they told her they'd get the truant officer after her, but Jane wasn't scared, Jane just kept walking."

"Well, you know she had a man over there," a neighbor named Shirley contributed; she was holding a package under her arm which I saw was addressed to Cleveland, Ohio. Her husband, Walter, shaking his head, but smiling, said: "Some kind of crazy guy they let out of Edgehill Farm. Now he's a born-again Christian. Jane grabbed him from the T & T and took him right to her house."

"Right to her house?"

"Born-again Christian," snorted Shirley, moving on with her package.

"Not really, though," someone else said. "He's got some peculiar—I don't know— beliefs about things."

And then there was a queer kind of theological discussion, right there in Moxie's. Shirley insisted she reads her Bible a little bit every night (although her husband Walter rolled his eyes, coughed, looked away.) "And I always thank God," one of the Welch women declared, "for his bounty. We've got food and a roof and we're comfortable. We've got pear trees in our yard. We've got our truck and some money in the bank account. We have our good health. God's been good to us."

I seldom interject in the general discussions at Moxie's. I'm a listener here. But I said, without really thinking: "What do you believe about people who don't have food and roofs?"

The town attitude, an instinctive defense, settled over the little group: tight-lipped, stiff-backed.

Walter: "They haven't got the Lord. That's what I think."

Shirley: "Well, that's *right. They're not walking in the grace of God."*

And I knew I should not pursue it, I should smile and nod, but I was driven by some need which I can now identify as a competitive one. Even a hostile one. "But does the grace of God really have much to do with food and houses and nice yards?"

Silence. I continued: "And, I mean, you mention good health . . . well, what does it mean when people are sick? What about when children are sick?"

"They're less fortunate than ourselves," Constance Welch said stridently, automatically and, I thought, unresponsively.

"We pray for them," said her daughter Fern.

I said: "But, maybe God really does not concern himself with earthly, worldly things like houses and cars. Or even health, even the physical body. Maybe God is only interested in the spirit."

Then a long, strained silence. I was prepared for an argument. I was prepared to interrogate this grim group about their simplistic beliefs, their professions of Christian goodness, and then slam them—in a humble fashion of course—with their ignorance, inconsistency, hypocrisy. Quote J.C., even—"Judge not, that ye be not judged." Matthew, chapter seven, verse one.

But I simply smiled. Who am I, anyway? Just a stranger. Caught up in my own judgments. A sensualist, a body and an ego, far distant from any knowledge of God. Playing some kind of game with the phonies of this town.

Their gossiping about Jane has become familiar to me by now; it is mostly comical. But then, later in the day, Cindy and I stood watching Jane's dilapidated old house—a place children are afraid of and grown-ups are fascinated by. (Which am I—child or grown-up?) And I found myself thinking of returning tomorrow to look at her house, and the next day, almost like a ritual. I don't understand what drives me, but I am, practically instinctively, indulging its lead. And I want to come the next day, and the next.

So I'm still here. I called my teaching assistant, told him to take care of some business for me. He asked if I would be back in time for the faculty meetings before classes begin, and I assured him I would, of course. Thinking, all the while, that I really don't know when I'll leave this place—appearing, probably, through the glass door of the Hotel Universe phone booth, rather sneaky, mischievous. Like a man lying to his wife.

Later—

Lunch with Ancer Peak. He was wearing—don't ask me why—a tropical-type shirt, with yellow-and-blue parrots on it. He's made his hair a lighter color. I was alone at the little diner in town, reading a student's paper on Paul Strand. So my mistake was sitting at a window table, because when Ancer Peak saw me, he bounded right in and took a seat. I had ordered a hamburger and Ancer asked for a salad plate.

"George is sick, have you heard?" he asked.

"No. I finally reached a friend of his, a woman named Elaine, who said he would call me back, but she didn't say anything. . . . How did you find this out?"

"Oh, George called me. From the hospital."

My ego, or vanity, or whatever, took immediate control. Who is this little monster, Ancer Peak?

Ancer Peak lighted one of his long, thin cigarettes. "Yes, they don't think it's too serious. Some kind of bronchial infection. He was having trouble breathing. I have his doctor's name and the phone number at his hospital room."

"Did he ask you to tell me about this?"

"Did he?" Ancer Peak feigned trying to recall. "I think he did—yes, he did ask me to let you know."

So now I felt relieved. George could only reach me through Ancer Peak as he knows I have no phone. Ancer Peak is too petty to admit that his only role is as messenger. Yes, so now I felt relieved, but fairly petty myself, all consumed with my status within this crisis, my access to the information, my dislike of Ancer Peak, and the feeling that George might care more for this despicable little rodent than for me. The real point is: George is ill. George is ill.

"Trouble breathing?" I asked.

"That's what I was told."

"God," I said, "I wonder . . ." I expected Ancer Peak to know what I was wondering. But he only blinked rapidly at me, waiting for me to finish the sentence. "I'm just wondering if it might not be HIV-related. I know George was tested, and it was negative; but that was at least two years ago."

"HIV? You mean, the thing that gives people AIDS?"

"Yes, of course."

"Is that possible?"

I repeated: "Is that possible?" *incredulously, not well concealing my impatience.*

Ancer Peak was looking over a newspaper he'd brought in with him. "Well, I don't know much about all of that."

"Listen——are you gay?" I was surprised at my own question. I never ask it; usually I know the answer so there is no reason to ask it; and in situations where I'm not sure, it hardly matters——like asking, Are you a Democrat, Are you married, Do you love the movies? Over a short time, generally, people reveal who they are, the facts, and the more intimate aspects of themselves. But I knew *this man was a homosexual and so what I was asking, with, admittedly, some hostility, was not actually if he was gay, but if he was alive, aware, connected, conscious, joined and caring and experienced? I was astounded and angry at his distance from such a crucial fact as AIDS——and, indeed, particularly because he is gay.*

"Well, yes, I am gay," he answered, as though the question had come entirely out of the blue.

"Do you know there's a plague going on?"

"Oh, yes, I see what you mean." He held a fork in the air, stabbed with boiled egg and lettuce and a black olive. "I haven't had much to do with it, really," said he, in that unreliable English accent of his. "I read about it in the papers. A couple of my old friends died of it. It hasn't hit me very hard, I'm happy to say." And the fork proceeded daintily into his mouth; he chewed untroubled.

Oh, so furious then, Meg. I felt like telling him everything about Mark——the really gruesome details. And then listing all the friends and fucks and acquaintances and co-workers, all the memorial services I've attended. All to communicate this fear about George.

But Ancer Peak, clearly, was unafraid. I'm a little jealous of that, I suppose. A bad cough and a hospital stay don't mean much to Ancer Peak. Neither do women writers (or probably women, for that matter). Neither does the sound of the waves at night or the gossip in the town. Neither do I matter to him.

I wanted to change the subject and considered telling him about Jane, my eavesdropping on her, my vision of her. I was moved for a moment to ask him if he'd heard the latest on Jane—her alliance with this mental patient, born-again Christian, whom Jane had shamelessly brought to her house. But Jane can't matter much to him either. What does mean something to Ancer Peak?

And then a queer inquiry popped into my frustrated, judgmental brain. I was going to ask: Do you believe in God? Where did that come from? I didn't ask it. I said I had work to do. I paid my check and left, walked back through the town. Passed Jane's. Melon rinds and ashes and soup cans and paper cups with faces drawn on them, scattered beneath her window. As though when Jane is through with something, or tired of it, she simply tosses it out her window.

Write to me from Mother's,

All my love,
Paul

7

Dear Meg:
Thank you for your last letter, and the new pictures of Audrey. Mother says you're off to New Mexico next month. I'm happy to think of you out of NYC, far away from Bert, back to a place I know you've always loved. And you have friends there, you're bound to find work. I want to say to you: Keep faith, don't give up. But you never give up. Your optimism is the most endearing, delicious thing about you. You're strong, and I envy that. You make decisions—they're too sudden sometimes, and sometimes maybe misguided and sometimes just right, but they are clear choices and you move ahead.

Not me. I'm frozen. I've always been paralyzed. In my tormented teens and twenties I spent many drunken nights sunk to the floor, curled in a corner, weeping, wondering what to do with my life. Through the night, smoking lousy pot and sniffling, and at daybreak I'd get some bright idea. To move to a new apartment; to leave my job; to go to school or quit school; to get rid of my boyfriend, or get back with the one I'd just dumped. Dry my tears, hopelessly, frustrated. I think the tears of my adolescence made permanent lines on my cheeks.

Do you remember the diving crisis at Red Feather Day Camp? You were so adept at the swimming pool. Not that you had anything like perfect form—the counselors were always barking at you to lower your head and bend your knees, and they'd roll their eyes when you'd bounce off the board and flail your way crookedly into the shining ice-blue water, emerge from the splash with a wild, satisfied grin. No, it was your fearlessness that impressed me. Destroyed me. Because when it was my turn to dive, I simply could not make myself do it. I stood there, not even on the diving board, but just at the cement-and-tile edge of the deep end. Utterly powerless—not meaning to refuse, but refusing. The counselors coaxed me, ordered me. They'd count to three; and there I'd stand, staring down. Other kids cajoled and teased. You'd be standing nearby, your arms folded across your flat chest, bits of crazy wet hair sticking out of your bathing cap. Was I embarrassing you, or were you trying to encourage me? Or just watching? The voices of the other kids grew louder and shamed me; but I stayed mute, stiff, dazed. I stared through the mirror surface of the water to the blue lines on the bottom of the pool. I could not fathom taking that jump. How lonely I was then. All summer, this futility and fear at the edge of the pool, and your loyalty, which was no comfort.

"Paul, did you do your diving today?" Mother asked at supper. "Meg, did Paul do his diving today?"

You looked at her with gravy on your chin. "Yeah. He did good."

"Well," Mother corrected. She believed you. You winked at me.

We're like characters in a myth, you and I, representing opposed views of life. If you have always believed that things would somehow work out, I've been unwaveringly sure they never would. You have some kind of trust in a reasonable world, in a life that progresses and makes sense and has meaning. Do you believe in God, Meg? Is that it? Is that how you always manage to take a deep breath and plunge in, and rise to the surface?

Admiringly,
Paul

8

Dear Meg:

It's five A.M. *the sky is white with fog at dawn, moist; my house is shadowed and chilly.*

The most extraordinary thing has happened. The most extraordinary, unbelievable thing I've ever seen or heard of has happened, right here, not an hour ago. A miracle.

I was sitting on the crooked wooden steps of the cabin. I was smoking a cigarette. I was watching the tops of the pine trees across the road; black crows were resting, then swooped away, and the trees swayed violently. Cindy was beside me.

I saw a car approaching. It got closer and I could see it was a taxi. Strange, way out here, a taxi. Closer, then it pulled up in front of my cabin and stopped. I stood up. Cindy stood up, too.

The back door of the taxi swung open, a leg stuck out, another leg, and then the whole person. It was Mark. Mark. A pudgy little cabdriver scurried to open the trunk and Mark pulled out his two suitcases and looked at me and smiled, walked toward me. And there he was.

I said, My God, my God, Mark, is it you? How can this be?

He seemed distracted, rushed. He carried his bags up the steps, into the cabin, and I followed.

But Mark, how can this be? How can this be possible?

I know it's a shock, *Mark told me.*

I said, But Mark, but Mark. You died.

I know, I know.

But you died. You were so sick. I came down to L.A. and you couldn't eat by yourself or move—

I remember, Paul, I know.

You couldn't even get out of bed or, or, or, or speak. *I thought I'd cry remembering. I do not like to think of Mark's last days. How angry and inward he had become. I am always so sure I'll cry with this remembrance, so I push the thoughts away.*

And then here was Mark, unpacking his shirts, bright yellow ones, vivid red ones. He was not even really looking at me. He was casual. He even laughed. Believe me, he said, I remember.

I went to your funeral, *I insisted. I was behind him, looking at his back, his neck, his blondish hair curled over his collar. Could this really be Mark, the same Mark? I moved toward him, around to see his face. I stood before him.*

Mark lifted his head and looked directly at me. He smiled. Watery blue eyes I'd known so many years. Weak chin and sour mouth. A funny-looking man. Mark always had been a funny-looking man. And then, over a quick, breathless year I had watched him deteriorate, and he never looked funny again, only in pain. He looked like suffering. I'd traveled to him once a month, then twice a month, then for weeks at a stretch. Kept a powerless eye on Mark as he slept, drugged. Scrubbed shit from the bathroom walls and floor. Once, delirious and so weak, he'd fallen in the tub at five A.M. and banged his head; he screamed and I screamed, the paramedics came. His shoulders and arms and face were covered with purple-yellow lesions, all different sizes, blood at the surface, like he was skinless.

Now, he was finished with his unpacking. I looked for the lesions—on his neck, his arms—and there were none. He put his living hand on my shoulder and said: I'm sorry about all this. It had to be done this way. It had to stay a secret until now. But I am alive, I'm really alive. Here I am.

Here he was, yes. How?

Someone saved my life, *he told me.*

Who?

I can't say any more right now. I'm fine, though. I'm cured. It's a miracle. And look— *From his shirt pocket, he brought a folded piece of paper which he tossed above his head, joyously, like it was a winning lottery ticket. When it had fluttered to the floor I bent down to look at it. A check, made out to Mark. The amount was $30,000.68. I could not discern the signature.*

All our troubles are over, *Mark yelled. He hurried into the kitchen then, opened the refrigerator.* What have you got to drink, Paul?

I followed him. So, Mark, I mean—you've been cured? Really cured? Yes.

They've found a cure? For AIDS?

Yes. No one knows yet. But they will know.

Breathless now, in suspense like at the movies: When? When?

Mark grabbed a pitcher of lemonade, removed its cap, drank a hearty and long gulp, and smiled. Tomorrow, *he said.*

Sometime later Mark was getting ready to sleep on the floor with a few blankets. I said, No, no, you will be in a draft, you'll get achy.

Those things don't matter anymore, Paul. I'm not sick now. I survived. I could lie down on a pile of mossy rocks, and I would sleep just fine.

Mossy rocks? No, but he was the fussiest, most fragile, weakest kind of being; every breeze cut him, every motion bruised him.

I started to cry, then. Frustrated weeping, like a little boy who cannot comprehend, who has been confused by a sudden unnatural sequence of events, who has been shocked away from certainty and is mostly angry.

Suddenly, then. No. It wasn't sudden. It was . . . time broke. And then David was here. You remember him Meg. My first boyfriend, all those years ago; the one who always called me neurotic? And something was making me jealous. I sat in a corner of George's cabin in a huge, overstuffed chair, like the one Dad used to have. My arms were folded over my chest. David was telling Mark about cute boys at a party. So I was jealous, angry, would not talk. Mark was laughing. Then he looked at me. Paul, oh, you're so serious all the time. Look, David, he's pouting. *David laughed and Mark laughed.*

Then I felt keenly guilty. Because here was Mark, alive and clean and smiling; and here I was, small and petty and jealous. These two were laughing and I was furious. These two were resurrected somehow; and my aloneness was resurrected too.

Meg? Did I say this was all a dream? Yes. This was all a dream. This morning, my eyes snapped open to stare at the edge of George's little bedside table; my fingers was gripping the handle of the drawer. The clock said 4:30 A.M. I lifted myself slowly to a sitting position, leaning back against the pillows which were damp from my sweat. My hair was wet and stuck to my forehead. I felt as though I'd been mercilessly beaten, and was alone now in the dark. I'd been mourning in my sleep. And was alone now in the dark and the truth was here. There's no Mark. He is dead. Thirty thousand dollars and sixty-eight cents? No. And AIDS is not over. Mark has no secret for me and for the world. David? I think he's in Canada, happy and dull. We exchange Christmas cards and I cannot even really remember his face. A smooth face, with lazy eyes . . . I cannot even remember our younger, more willing bodies in our bed, or that voice of his that an adolescent me waited for and hated and cried about.

Grief in dreams. Mourning who I loved and the way I loved, because all of that is gone.

I wish I had a phone. To call a friend and verify real life. I wake up to the sounds of now—this even wind before daybreak. Disoriented, uncertain. Whispering: What year is this? What era? Are we still in trouble? And in a moment I know, Yes, yes, we're still in trouble. No miracle.

PART IV

I

In the autumn, the leaves of the trees did not change color here, but
certain flowers bloomed with astonishing suddenness—sunflowers and
pink lilies—and the fog washed over the land colder, earlier, and for
a longer time. Windows had been kept wide open during the still
summer, but now they were closed, for huge ocean winds would sweep
through the dirty town.

Jane's front door stood fully open, and there were paint cans and
brushes and rollers spread out on her porch. She had hired some high
school boys to give her house a fresh coat; when it was done it would
be a muted, creamy yellow with a dark green trim.

On a chilly, sunny morning, three people stood waiting on Jane's
porch, a respectable distance from the open door. They were a man, a
woman, and a young girl. The girl, fifteen or sixteen, was seated in a
wheelchair.

"Should we just walk in?" the woman wondered.

The man said: "No, no. We'll wait here. Don't go just walking into
people's houses."

This was a plain family, from a town in Oregon. The woman held
a maroon imitation-leather handbag in front of her; the man wore a hat.
The girl in the wheelchair wore eyeglasses whose frames were slightly
too large for her narrow face; she twisted a rope of her hair—gorgeous
auburn hair—with two fingers; she squinted to stare into Jane's house,
down the narrow corridor to the kitchen at the other side.

They stayed here, in a line, rigid and dumb, expectant. Finally, the
girl said: "Oh, there's someone. There's someone. That must be her."
The man pulled at the brim of his hat and stood straighter; the woman
tugged at her jacket, then quickly smoothed the girl's hair.

Jane appeared from the kitchen and was walking down the hall, toward them. She was wearing a peach-colored dress with white collar and cuffs, and flat shoes. Her hair was fixed in a loose bun at the back of her head. She was smiling at the three on the porch as she came to greet them; but Jane smiled shyly, as her teeth were still discolored and embarrassing to her.

She arrived at her front door and briefly looked at each of the three people before her, directly, into their eyes.

"We're the Overbecks?" the man offered, phrasing his statements as questions. "We called? Last Tuesday?"

"Yes, of course," said Jane. "Oh, please, oh, excuse all this mess on the porch. Come in, come this way." She swept her arm gracefully, urging them forward. The woman followed Jane inside, and the man pushed the girl's wheelchair.

"All the way to the kitchen," said Jane, motioning them. The kitchen, too, had been painted and the shelves freshly papered, the boxes and piles of newspapers removed. It was a bright room now, airy and clean. When they were all settled around Jane's teak kitchen table, Jane asked if any of them would like some tea. The Overbecks did not answer.

Mrs. Overbeck looked at Jane, her eyes rimmed with moist redness. "We've come such a long way to see you," she said softly.

"I know," Jane said

"Oh, yes," said the man after clearing his throat. "We heard about you, of course. And my wife got it into her head to come down and see you. I must tell you, I was not in favor of this. I'm the skeptical type."

Mrs. Overbeck slapped her fingers lightly on her husband's sleeve, then leaned forward, her bosom pressed against the table edge, toward Jane. "He is. Del *is* the skeptical type. He doesn't believe in anything."

Jane smiled that withholding, rather sweet smile she had lately developed. "That's fine. Neither do I."

Suddenly, the girl in the wheelchair spoke, rather loudly. "Well, if *you* don't believe it, and *we* don't believe it, what are we doing here anyway?" Her brow was tense.

"Ivy," whispered the mother, and the father again cleared his throat. But the girl was staring hard at Jane.

Jane held her hand up. "It's all right. It's fine. I'm not asking anyone to believe anything." She glanced at each one of these people, deliberately but warmly. "I don't understand myself what's going on. All I know—" Jane abruptly stopped speaking. She pushed back a bit of hair that had come undone. She rose then and stood at the window, holding the edge of her new, sheer white curtain, her back to the Overbecks.

"Well, we heard you were healing people," Mrs. Overbeck said, sounding on the verge of tears. "We heard some crippled people and people who couldn't hear or see had come to you. And you had completely healed them. That's the truth, isn't it?"

Jane gave a short laugh, then turned around. "Yes. That's the truth. It started with my own little boy, my little Russell—" And now she moved about the room, passing fingers lightly over the clock on a shelf above the stove, over the counter, seeming distracted. She gazed for a moment at the framed photograph she had hung beside the hutch: a picture of her mother and sisters. "See, Russell was very sick. No one could cure him, no one even could say what was wrong with him. Russell became worse and worse. And I didn't know what to do. I didn't know *what* to do, and so I became very desperate." Now she stood still in the center of the room. She looked directly at Mrs. Overbeck. "Desperate. There was drinking. Men. I did not eat, I did not sleep. I was so afraid for Russell and for myself. And so I became lost. You can understand that."

The woman nodded.

"I was at a crossroads," Jane told them. "I was at a turning point in my life. One way was despair, fear, abandonment. One way was love, happiness, forgiveness, peace. I was at a crossroads and I had to choose."

Mrs. Overbeck pushed herself forward, so that she was perched on the edge of her seat. "It was Jesus."

Her husband reprimanded her with a bark of her name—"Felicity" —and a stern glance. Then he asked Jane, doubtfully: "Well, was it Jesus?"

Jane withdrew a partly crumpled pack of cigarettes from the pocket of her skirt. She lit one and blew smoke out in a soft, shapeless cloud. She resumed her seat at the table. She shrugged her shoulders. She was smiling and warm. "I don't know. And I can't really talk about it. All

I know is that one day I was suffering and in pain and afraid; and the next day I was offered grace. And a gift. A gift to heal other people who are suffering and in pain and afraid."

"And you cured your little boy?"

Jane did not answer.

"Yes, but how exactly does this work?" Mr. Overbeck wanted to know.

"I can't say. I don't know."

Mrs. Overbeck whispered: "Jesus is the only thing that works."

Jane had heard the woman's words. "Maybe you're right. All I know is that it's something in my touch. I start by listening, very hard. I listen, I listen, and then something in my touch erases pain, breaks it."

They were all silent for a moment. A breeze swept the curtain into the room and Jane reached behind her and closed the window.

Mrs. Overbeck spoke quickly, stridently. "Ivy fell off a trampoline seven years ago. A trampoline at her school. And she's been paralyzed like this ever since. Paralyzed from the chest down. But she can move one hand."

"Well, let's find out a few things," interjected Mr. Overbeck. "First of all: What is the fee for your services?"

"No fee," Jane replied.

Mrs. Overbeck was suddenly flooded with emotion and let out a sob. She swiftly brought a handkerchief from her handbag and held it to her nose. "Excuse me, please," she whispered.

"No fee?" inquired Mr. Overbeck.

"No."

"And do you think you can help my daughter?"

Jane faced the girl. Jane's intense eyes examined the girl's thin face, her hair, moved smoothly and deliberately over the girl's seated figure. "Yes," said Jane finally. "Yes, I think I can."

Ivy's glasses had slipped down her nose and she pushed them up with her thumb. "Well, what *I* want to know is what about your kid? What about Russell? What happened to him?"

Jane turned her head, looking through the window over her right shoulder. Mr. and Mrs. Overbeck followed her gaze, then rose to go to the window. They each pulled back a corner of the curtain. Ivy lifted her chin, strained her neck, trying to see.

Outside, Russell was seated on a black rubber truck tire that was suspended with rope from a sturdy tree limb; he was pushing with his bare feet against the tree's fat trunk, and swinging wildly, hugging the tire, leaning back his head. His mouth was open, his hair blown by the breeze. He pushed himself and swung, pushed himself harder and swung further, and as the tire began to rotate in a swifter, more exhilarating circle, the laughing boy seemed only a blur.

Mrs. Overbeck was crying. Her husband gravely watched the boy outside. Jane rose and stood behind Ivy's wheelchair.

"He's really cured?" the girl asked.

Jane put her hands on the girl's shoulders. "He's very happy, dear. And so am I."

2

Dear Meg:

Finally there's word about George. Ancer Peak left a note under my door asking me to stop by. I bundled up—it's getting much colder here now—and walked up the hill to his house. He invited me in, distractedly. He had moist, red-rimmed eyes, from all the pot he smokes, I guess. "I'm just packing," he said, in his put-on accent. "I'm going to fly to Boston this evening."

"Is George worse?" I wanted to know, watching his back as he scurried from drawer to drawer and piled shirts in a suitcase open on the bed.

"No, actually," said Ancer Peak. "He's doing much better. Weak, a little weak of course. But"—and now he turned to face me, as though to relate some difficult news—"they think it might be AIDS."

This seemed such an obscenely obvious declaration, like remarking that it sure is windy while a cyclone is sweeping away your town. He blinked at me, pursed his lips; he expected some reaction from me. But I only felt frustrated, and I repressed any expression of that. I wanted to ask him why he was flying off to see George, of what possible use did he think he could be? He, with virtually no understanding of or experience with AIDS. And then, too, I feel left out. I told Ancer Peak to please give George my warmest greetings, to say that I will see him soon, that I am willing to help in any way I can. Ancer Peak smiled sweetly and assured me he'd deliver my message. I went home, fuming, dragging Cindy so hard she actually choked out a dry hack. "Sorry, sorry," I told her, loosening her collar. She is accepting my apologies more graciously these days. Cindy likes me, I'm sure of it. An hour ago, I saw Ancer Peak's wretched yellow convertible speeding down the road, out of town.

Evening—
The latest news about Jane is truly sublime. Unfortunately, I'm having trouble piecing together the whole story. Apparently, Jane has undergone a complete change of character. No longer pale and fierce, she's now rosy-cheeked, serene. Furthermore, she is convinced, and so are some others, that she had developed—or been granted, or discovered, or whatever—a kind of divine power to heal the sick. All of this has occurred in the last couple of weeks. It's a spiritual thing. That vitriolic town woman, Shirley, humpfed: "Yes. The Miracle of Our Lady of the T & T Cocktail Lounge."

But this information is so powerful and shocking that people are not able to keep quiet. It is the talk of the town.

"Well, she did cure her own little boy," I heard someone insist. And the cynical reply: "But, the way I heard it, her little boy didn't have not one thing wrong with him." "Yes," someone else offered, laughing, "in that case, I could have cured him."

I'm sensing that Jane's new life extends beyond ordinary juicy gossip—the shocking, the inappropriate, the sexual. Because it is abstract. Jane's transformation does not have the simple vitality of an action or a word that can be judged, scorned, doubted; Jane is different than she used to be, which is fundamentally threatening. If Jane's character was part of how the town saw itself, part of the identity of these people, she has upset all of that.

That old house of Jane's is certainly reflecting her spiritual growth. She's having it painted. She's planted pansies and geraniums and lined the front walk with marigolds in tin coffee cans. I got a look at Jane, only yesterday. And it's true—she does seem more serene. She strode breezily along High Street, holding hands with little Russell, who seemed in perfectly fine spirits and health. No beret now, or dirty, dark dresses. Her hair was loose; she wore a cream-colored blouse and a pale blue skirt.

The two of them were singing. Jane had a folder under her arm and a roll of masking tape over her wrist, like a bracelet. She was stepping inside each office and store and asking the proprietor's permission to tape a poster on the window. I was at Moxie's for cigarettes when she and Russell came in.

"I just want to put up one of my posters," she said to the ladies at the counter, meeting their eyes directly, smiling broadly. "That's all right with you, isn't it?"

Both women nodded.

"Thanks so much," Jane said sweetly, but not disingenuously. She took a yellow flyer from her folder and affixed it with tape to the glass pane on the door.

"Another one of your meetings?" one of the clerks asked, in an inscrutable monotone.

"That's right," Jane answered, smoothing the poster. She turned around to face the women. "People keep wanting me to do it, and so . . . so, I do it." She gave a charming, easy shrug. Then she looked at me. I believe it was the very first time she's ever really looked at me. "Morning," she said on her way out. Russell chased after her.

Whatever explanation there may be for this transformation, there is no doubt about its extremity. That vulgar, resentful, dark creature I have been observing now for a month or more has vanished, and in her place is a new Jane: confident, appealing, not too soft or too loud.

The folks at Moxie's, I have to assume, are for some reason threatened by Jane's incredible alteration. Certainly they are cynical. But I am delighted and intrigued. I walked over to take a look at the poster. It read:

ARE YOU UNHAPPY? SICK OR IN PAIN?

ARE YOU LOST?

ARE YOU LOOKING FOR LOVE, HEALTH, PEACE OF MIND?

DO YOU WANT TO CHANGE YOUR LIFE?

And then there was a date given for Jane's next "meeting," to be held at her home, on her front porch, at dawn. At the bottom of the poster were the words: "No money or other form of payment is expected, and none will be accepted."

What do you make of this? I'm flabbergasted. I left the store and saw Jane and her little boy cheerfully gliding down the street, practically skipping. And then heads were popping out of windows and doorways, to watch them.

"I was lonely once," she said. She crossed her arms over her chest, lifted her head toward the new sun. Her eyes were closed. "Yes, I was lonely. I was miserable and empty. I walked through this world starving, suffering, sick. And then I was lifted up. I found something."

"Jesus!" someone called up.

Jane laughed, heartily and happily. "Well, Jesus is a very lovely wish." And books and saints were lovely wishes. Her mother had wished those wishes. Jane laughed again and, again, there was no trace of that old bitterness people had always heard in her laughter.

She opened her eyes, brought her arms down to her sides, looked over the assembled guests. Today there were ten of them. But sometimes to Jane it seemed there were fifty or a thousand, sometimes only one. Beside her on the porch was young Ivy Overbeck, standing fully erect, without benefit of wheelchair or crutch or cane.

"I *still* don't believe it," the girl had told Jane, even after Jane had eased her from her chair and shown her she could walk. "I see it, I feel it, but I *still* don't believe it."

"That's fine, Ivy. That's just fine."

"There must be some good explanation."

"Yes, there must be," Jane agreed.

Ivy had walked up and down the porch steps, several times. "No. I can't believe it," was her firm conclusion.

And Jane said: "I love you."

Miss Shrike had called Jane from San Francisco last week. "I swear to God, I swear to God they found these tumors in my breast, three tumors, and then they said the cancer had spread, and they said they thought I'd only have a few months to live. And I came to you, Jane, and you healed me. And when I went back, I swear to God, the doctors said they couldn't find those tumors anymore. They said they couldn't find any cancer anywhere in me. I swear to God."

And the man with AIDS had written to her. Jane had pressed her fingers against six lesions on his face, and the lesions were gone now, gone. He had friends; he wanted to know, could he send his friends?

A husband and wife, young people who lived up in the hills, came to Jane; dope addicts, miserable and hopeless and angry. Jane had seen them yesterday in the hardware store, choosing saw blades. The husband greeted Jane, held her hand warmly. The wife seemed shy, stood apart. But as Jane was leaving, the wife rushed up to Jane, kissed Jane's cheek. "Thank you," said the young woman, and she was crying.

There were questions whispered in her head, deep inside, behind her ears. *Is it a trick, Jane? Or is it real? How do you do it? Does it come from your mind? Your spirit?* Jane shrugged her shoulders, smiled, all heart and humility; she did not know the answers.

Now, on a sunny, chilly morning, Jane stood on her newly repaired porch, before those assembled on the front walk. She could see that some were suspicious of her, and some were even there to mock her. But she felt no pain.

She had so much she wanted to say to the people. Jane closed her eyes; the sun beat steadily against her cheeks, as though there were two strong, hot hands holding her. The soft coils of her clean hair felt pleasantly hot against her neck. She heard Russell's tiny laugh far away. She heard, from long ago, the serious, uncaring voice of a doctor through the phone: *I don't understand you, Jane.* She heard that stranger's voice, gentle and low. She heard her own echoing cries in the wide, sad night: *I'll take you people on if I have to! . . . I don't believe you. . . . Who am I? . . .*

So there were things she wished to say to these people. She had a story to tell, of how she'd come from an old dismal place to this new shining one; but the sounds and images flew by her too fast, and through her, escaping words. Jane had that same curious, funny feeling she'd had every day now—that she knew more than she could ever say. And it truly was a funny feeling to her, and she laughed a bit. Then she opened her eyes.

There were the tops of heads—ladies' flowered hats, men's hair blown by the wind. Doubtful expressions, and hopeful ones. She looked for her stranger; he was not there. Would she even recognize him?

"If someone would like to come forward," Jane said, "I am ready now."

There was silence. She recognized a few of the townspeople; they gazed at her with palpable disbelief. Then she saw an older man, a farmer. He was rail thin, dressed in overalls and a faded plaid shirt. He was not from around here. He was looking directly at Jane's eyes. She smiled at him, but he did not smile. He was scowling. Jane extended a hand. His skeptical expression did not change as he stepped up on to Jane's porch.

"What is it?" asked Jane.

The man was quite tall and Jane found that her eyes were level with his sunburnt, creased neck. He had a bit of fine white hair, barely covering his red scalp. "This eye can't see," he said. He held a dirty finger under his left eye.

She had to reach up to him, he was so much taller than she. She cupped her right hand gently over the man's bad eye. She closed her own eyes.

I am the poor in spirit, she heard her own desperate, furious voice say, and it chilled Jane; but then she smiled because that voice was no longer hers. I am happy now. Now I am free.

As always, when she did her healings, time was lost to her, and any sense of where she was or what she was doing. She was conscious only of sounds, but even these were indistinct, distorted, like a record played at high speed. Sounds that made no sense. Wind spoke. To Jane, people who were crying seemed to be laughing. The violent surf sounded like childrens' toy bells.

Her neighbor, the man who played piano, whom Jane had cursed and hated. One day Jane saw him standing outside the bank. Tiny, oddly shaped man. He waved to someone. He was grinning. He called out: "Good morning!" But Jane heard other words; Jane heard him say: *I'm afraid I'm afraid I'm afraid,* a breathless, pitiful incantation.

There was a man who'd only been in town some weeks now, or maybe a month. He walked a shaggy, mean little dog. The man seemed content, striding along easily, puffing a cigarette, with a camera over his shoulder; but Jane heard him weeping, heard deep, uncontrollable sobs. And Jane could hear that little dog humming a sweet tune.

Jane opened her eyes. There she was, standing on her toes, her hand over this man's eye. People in her pretty yard, watching and waiting. Jane took away her hand. She never knew what the result would be. She had no understanding of her own power, and no command of it. It was not a thing she summoned and used with awareness or will. It was as mysterious to Jane as it was to everyone else.

Each time Jane touched a person, and that person could hear or walk or speak or see, there would be joyful, amazed, alarmed cries all around her. Families and neighbors, and the person who was healed, would be swept up in their jubilation. Long years of grief for some sick person would be released, quite suddenly, and confusion followed. And some-one would say: "A miracle." But for Jane it was never a miracle; only a surprise.

So the old farmer blinked. He squinted. He brought his rough, red hand up to his face and placed it flat over his right eye, the good one. The man stood still, kept his head straight, but that other eye stared at Jane, looked her up and down. He was seeing her. He did not seem grateful, particularly; he even seemed angry. He had his sight back, but seemed to resent it. Jane smiled at him. He turned, his hand still covering the healthy eye, and looked out at the faces in the crowd, then far off to the road. He saw.

Jane held his shoulders, lifted herself up against his face and whis-pered in his ear: "I hope you can be happy."

It was one thing for Jane to have found God. But this healing of people's afflictions was quite another matter. Some people in the town thought she should be stopped. A few people even thought that it wasn't God in Jane, but the devil. Ancer Peak went around talking about psychic researchers in Los Angeles. "They have tests," he told some people at Moxie's. "They have scientific tests to measure some-one's psychic abilities. Jane should go down there and let them study her."

No one said much directly to Jane. Really, as people had always shunned and hawk-eyed her, they still did. Jane's happiness now was apparent, just as her unhappiness had been, all those years. It was not the facts that troubled the town, but the meaning behind the facts. Was she taking drugs? some people wondered. Or did she get converted by a preacher? And some, more generous perhaps, would declare that Jane was happy now because her little boy, her little Russell, was cured of his sickness. But he had never *had* any sickness.

As people did not say much to Jane, she still also stayed to herself. She did enroll her boy in school. The principal said that they were already into the semester, that Russell would be behind in his studies. Jane said she knew that, and she was sorry for all the bad words. She said she trusted the teachers with Russell and was sure he would do just fine. Kissed her boy's forehead. "I love you, Russell," she said to him, holding his soft ears, smiling down at him.

"She's into this healing business for the money," it occurred to someone one day. "That's it, she's aiming to get some money from all this."

"But she's not charging people anything. . . ."

"She will. You wait. Anything we know for sure about Jane it's how cheap she is."

"That's true."

But a magazine in San Francisco had heard about Jane and sent a woman reporter up to meet with her. Jane, smiling, politely declined an interview. The reporter went to talk to others in the town; but when Shirley and Walter and the Welches and the rest heard that Jane did not wish to speak, they stayed silent as well.

4

Dear Meg—

Long time since I've written.

I've gotten lost up here. Or maybe stuck. Can't seem to leave. I look in the dusty bathroom mirror and am horrified: Is that scraggly man me? I've become very neglectful of myself. Long, reddish-brown hair, whiskers. I've disintegrated into some kind of flower child—and I have that same sad-happy look those types used to have. The eyes are mine, I think, but disconnected from what they used to see so clearly. My eyes are seeing other things now.

What has it been—about a month and a half? I'm receiving thick envelopes from school, with URGENT stamped on them. I've thrown them, unopened, on a pile next to the wood stove. Soon I'll just burn them.

Even Mother sent me a note: "Your father and I are worried about you." Which made me so angry, and I can't say why.

I am not in some kind of rebellion up here in the woods, Meg. And it isn't that I am enjoying myself so fully that I'm just selfishly tossing away my former life. No—I'm quite literally unable to go home. I do think about it. I envision packing my things, shaving my face, putting on city clothes, hopping in my beat-up orange VW and heading back to where I belong. Good-bye to this ominous, gorgeous coastal town. I think about it. But the faces of my friends, the restaurants I know, my office and books and students—all of this I can't seem to locate anymore. My life was extreme, exalted and scary and exciting and amusing; but even so, it was innocent. Clicking cameras and gossiping. Ambition. Romantic tangles. Grudges.

Now, up here, I am humbled. Because I'm alone. Do you see, Meg? I've been thinking this is the first time I've ever really been alone, but that's not true, not true. I've always been alone.

Just after dawn, I sit barefoot on the porch, sipping black coffee, watching the fog. In the morning, I will take my hike through the overgrown trails, across the rocks, down to the water. I've come to know my way, exactly like the Indians of our grade-school picture books—I recognize every bend and raised root, I know the muddy patches and brambles. I step lightly. I hear every sound, and make no sound myself.

I've stopped carrying my cameras now, Meg. I don't even carry a bag. I am frequently wearing the clothes of the day before. I'll bring an apple and a jar of water with me, descend into my new home of wildness and insects and animal rustling and wind. My silver dead trees. My bird sounds. And by the time I've reached the water's edge, I'm in tears, Meg, simply to see and hear and be this close to my tide. The emotional state is indescribable. No photograph could possibly capture it, no letter to you could make it clear. It's as though, with my first step, I am embraced by some giant, gentle hand, and it pushes me forward; but it is a rough, terrifying embrace, which wants me raw, without intellect, without ego, without claims or regrets, without even a vision. Vision is all I ever believed I had. But now I'm only blood, water, heart, breath. My convictions are coarse. My desire is shapeless. What I know has been subjected to a process of transliteration, and is unfamiliar now. So I'm in inexplicable tears. My tide . . . Here I am, undetermined, stripped of all attitude or approach to life, of sentiment and judgment. Disengaged from what has always been apparent to me. Suffocating in this clean, cool air. Is this death, or renewal?

I guess I'm falling apart.

Love,
Paul

In the story Jane was reading aloud, a little boy lived with his big sister in a cabin in the woods; they were orphans.

"What's that—orphans?"

"It means their parents have died."

Jane and her boy were curled into each other against some cushions before the steady fire. Jane had made cocoa; now it was lukewarm. The book was an old one, originally her mother's, of fairy stories and biographies of famous people, with many illustrations and some color plates. She continued to read. The boy and girl saw a kitten in a tree. They saved the kitten. And when the kitten grew into a majestic cat, with thick, soft fur, it came to have some magical powers.

"Where are people when they're dead? They're not here anymore, but where do they go?"

"I don't know, Russell. No one knows." She closed the book, held her thumb inside to mark their place.

"But it's sad when people die?"

"It's sad because we miss them. But for them—maybe it isn't so sad."

"Does everyone die?"

"Yes, Russell."

Jane knew that man was outside her window. He'd gotten bolder in recent days, or simply more curious. He used to stand at the end of her yard, looking in her kitchen window. Now she knew he was on her porch, looking in at her and Russell and their fire. He did not make a sound.

Jane closed her eyes. She could hear his breathing, then. That man was very tired. That man was disabled with exhaustion. His little dog sat up on the road, waiting.

"Shall we go back to our story? Do you want to hear more about the magic cat?"

Russell sat up suddenly, held onto his mother's elbow, looked at her wide-eyed. "If someone dies, does that mean we never get to see them again, ever?"

Jane did not answer. She smiled at the boy, slid her fingers through his hair and placed her palm against his heated cheeks. The child's brow contorted into an adult's anxious concern. Then his expression relaxed and he smiled. Jane pressed two fingers against his nose; he drew back, laughing.

"Time to tickle Russell?" Jane asked, with mock menace.

"No, no, no," the boy protested, but flung himself against her breast. Jane held her strong arms around him, rocked him, wriggled her fingers against his belly in play, and Russell laughed; he said for her to stop, but laughed long and loud until he was tired, collapsed in his mother's lap.

She did not read more. She let Russell drift to sleep as she smoothed his black hair, shining in the firelight. She did not glance at the window; she had a feeling the man was gone.

6

Dear Meg—

Really winter now. No snow, but biting cold. I'm wearing two pairs of thick socks and gloves. Hard rain crashes against the windows. I sit on a pile of blankets beside the wood stove, smoking cigarettes, drinking tea.

Got your last letter. Sorry it takes me so long to write back. Yes, I'm sure you are getting all kinds of advice and recriminations and phony encouragement from the sidelines. You ask me to be gentle with you, respect your decision.

Well, what is the story? Let me outline the story. You loved a man and married him. You had a child. The man became cruel. He hit you. You were miserable, you felt alone. You left him. And now you have gone back to him.

The way I see it—from this cabin on the coast—it is not even necessary for me to respect your decision. I have no opinion. It is a scary, miraculous transformation in me, to have no opinion. Contrary to my strong ideas and outrage when I first learned that Bert had hurt you, and how he'd hurt you, now I am strangely detached. Your choices are not good or bad, smart or dumb, healthy or unhealthy. They're just your choices. Life is like my winding, dangerous, exhilarating path through the woods. (No, no—I can't philosophize either.)

But you are back with Bert. You wrote that *"marriage involves endless compromising."* I'm suddenly remembering, with astonishing vividness, Aunt Sophie and Jack. No one ever called him Uncle Jack, as though denying him his title would express implicitly what could not be openly said: he was not family, he was not loved. I remember Mother taking me to visit them. It was a long drive, along straight, dull county roads, past those post-WWII tiny box houses. I asked Mother: "How come the houses are so small but the yards are so big?"

This is years and years ago, of course, before Mother said she'd never speak to her sister again. I was six or seven years old, and Danny and Sue are between you and me in age. They were standing on the cement porch when we arrived, looking glum. Those kids were always quiet when I saw them, but it seemed to me, even back then, that that was not their true temperament—they had been bullied into good manners and clean hands and faces.

The living room was cramped and cluttered, and Aunt Sophie apologized. "Excuse all of this mess, here, let me clear some room, I'm sorry about these toys, I tell the children, I'm sorry."

Mother said: "Stop saying you're sorry, Soph. It's fine." Of course she did not sound like it was fine. She lifted a stack of magazines from the corner of a messy old sofa and plopped herself down.

Then Jack was in the doorway between the living room and kitchen. "Get this stuff out of here," he said to his children, and Danny and Sue swiftly, silently followed his order—grabbing skates, stuffed animals, dolls, puzzle pieces—and disappeared into some other part of the house. It was as though bandits had come through.

I looked at Aunt Sophie. She smiled at me. Her eyes always looked watery. "How do you like school, Paul?"

"Fine."

"Oh, that's good. What's your favorite thing to do in school?" She patted her sticky, shiny high hairdo. Her voice was pitifully strained and tense. Her watery eyes reflected excruciating fragility and hunger.

"I don't know. When they read to us. I'm learning how to read."

"Oh, isn't that wonderful?"

Then Jack came into the room, sat down in an armchair across from us. Mother winced. That chair—all of their furniture—had belonged to her mother. Mother did not like the contrast: brutish Jack putting his tumbler of scotch on her mother's rosewood table and leaving a ring; sloppy, rude Jack draping his leg over the arm of her mother's antique upholstered chair. Jack took up space, or seemed to. He wasn't all that big, probably, but he sighed loudly, walked heavily, he was an intrusion. When he smoked a cigarette, he exhaled a thick, dusty cloud, which Aunt Sophie would wave away with her plump hand while she smiled patiently—she was practiced in being unoffended. When he begrudgingly offered Mother a drink, it was a booming interruption. And he never even glanced at me.

Mother reacted to this oaf by turning her shoulder to him and not looking at him once. Aunt Sophie peered at her husband continually, gauging his responses, signaling with her dark penciled eyebrows that she would gladly get him another drink, or empty the ashtray, or fix him a sandwich. Even as a little boy, I could see that Aunt Sophie was terrified in her own home. I did not know exactly what was wrong there— violence, indecision, threats, lies—but I knew it was wrong to be terrified in your own home.

"I'm so happy to see you, Paul. And you've grown so much." These are, of course, the typical, corny declarations of relatives, but they felt pleasing and warm. Aunt Sophie never seemed contrived to me. She was oddly distant from her own communications, but I thought her interest and enthusiasm were quite genuine. She had a huge, gorgeous smile, but it could disappear in a second if she heard a sharp sound in the kitchen, if a noisy car went past, if one of her kids sneezed. When she brought a cigarette to her lips, it trembled the tiniest bit between her fingers. It seemed she had other things on her mind. I guess that's from Mother, who always said: "Aunt Soph has a lot on her mind." This statement served as a kind of explanation of the woman for me—and also, "Aunt Soph is very nervous"; "Aunt Soph's going through some difficult times." Mother seemed to have a sensible and compassionate attitude toward her big sister, and I never noticed that her kind words were uttered through clenched teeth. Did you?

So that when the sisters finally broke, I was truly shocked. By then I was fourteen or so. Mother had gone for a weekend with her sister, but she returned home early. She and Dad had private talks. She told Dad: "That's it!" and he held up his hands and said: "All right, all right." What had happened?

On Sunday, Mother was at the kitchen table, holding the phone, her legs crossed at the knee and her foot tapping the leg of her chair. She said nothing, just listened. She looked at the ceiling, her lips were tight. I could hear Aunt Sophie's voice, though no words, through the phone—some kind of desperate explanations to Mother, pleading. I hung around, making a sandwich, pouring some juice, to hear what Mother would say, so I could know what all this was about. But she said nothing. The high-pitched, electronic cracklings from the phone ceased. Mother sat there for a moment. Then she hung up.

I know Mother struggled with her judgments, her anger, her resolve. Over the years I heard her tell her friends that she simply could not accept her sister's passivity; that *year after year, Aunt Sophie allowed that lazy, cruel man to brutalize her and her children; that she, Mother, could not bear to hear ever again about the fights, the police reports, the bruises, only to have this violence in their lives forgotten about, covered over, denied. She saw her sister as profoundly weak—which is, for Mother, a moral issue. And that weakness she perceived was intolerable.*

When I was much older I challenged Mother a bit: "Actually, thinking about it, Aunt Sophie is also incredibly strong. Can you see that?"

"No," was Mother's response. "And I really adored my sister. All our lives. I really love her. But if I'd been in her shoes, I'd have been out of that house and away from that man decades ago."

She always tenses at any mention of Aunt Sophie or those kids. She cries sometimes, too, but angrily. It is a loss for her, I know, but she cannot fully feel that loss because of her righteousness. She interpreted, classified, and condemned her sister's choices, her sister's way of life and loving; and then she felt her deepest pain; and then she lost.

Do you see what I'm getting at, Meg?

Dear Meg—
More bad dreams. Every night. But maybe I shouldn't call them bad—they're scary. One of a barn burning at midnight. Wild, white flames. Deer running to escape. Another of trees falling, thundering and cracking to the ground while I watch, helpless, my hands in my coat pockets, afraid the trees will hit me.

Still not sure of my plans. Please write to me. Write to me today.

Paul

Dear Sister—
Hallowe'en is coming. Ghosts made of pillows and sheets with black painted eyes are hanging from tree limbs, floating eerily in the strong breezes. Children will stand around tiny, contained bonfires, hypnotized by jumping flames and dreams of ghouls, witches, monsters.

Terrible news. George has gone blind now. Ancer Peak told me this and I kept trying to call George, kept walking down to the Hotel Universe, getting more and more frantic. Image of George with dark glasses, like black circles over his eyes, arms stretched out, feeling his way through a hospital corridor. Finally, when I dialled the number, George answered.

Hello? Hello, George, it's Paul.

You're shouting. Don't shout. I've gone blind, not deaf.

George, I am so sorry to hear about this.

Yes. Yes, well. I really don't want to talk about it.

Cindy misses you.

I have to stay here for some time now, Paul. At least another three weeks. They're going to try laser surgery.

Is it—will they—do they think they can help you?

Slim chance.

Are you—?

I was going to ask him if he was all right. That's dumb. In good spirits? Holding up?

I'm furious. That's what I am.

I understand.

I'm angry and exhausted and ready to call it quits.

I can . . . I can understand that. Really. Is there anything I can do here, George? What about the cabin?

The cabin . . . When you're ready to go, just lock the door.

I did not want to mention Cindy again. Don't worry about anything.

Paul, I have to go now.

I love you, George. I really love you.

Good-bye, Paul.

He did not say he loved me. I wanted George to say that he loved me, too. I hung up and cried. The bellboy stared at me, then looked away.

I pulled Cindy up onto the bed with me that night, wrapped her in the quilt; she whimpered, fussed, hopped off the bed and strolled to her little cushion in the corner. She abandoned me.

Dear Meg:

Late night. Fearful, again. I think I am a big fraud. Always have been. Unconsciously a fraud, though—that is, I don't misrepresent myself for practical gain, to manipulate. But the fraudulence is more inside than outside anyway. What I say and how I act are not really me. I am not who I think I am.

Jane was sitting at her kitchen table. There was a candle in a brown bottle, but no other light. Jane held her hands on the top of her head. Slid the hands down her face, the fingers spread wide. To her breasts. Then she leaned back her head, stretching her neck, and she was smiling, her eyes were closed.

The plum tree outside her window was whispering to her, in a woman's voice: *What is it, Jane? How can it be?*

"I don't know," she answered softly.

Have you found God?

Jane shook her head. She looked at the bare branches, purple-black against the night sky. "Are you my mother?"

She rose and walked to the kitchen sink. She filled a glass with water from the tap and drank it in one gulp, holding her head far back, standing with her feet apart, one arm extended, like a dancer posing.

Then she heard piano music. A popular tune she remembered. She knew some of the words and sang along softly, and moved in a small circle, airily, dreamily, holding folds of her skirt.

I remember that song, too. *What is this thing called love? This funny thing called love.* I realized quite suddenly that I was cold out there. My hands were jammed in my coat pockets, my shoulders lifted. I turned and saw Cindy's silhouette some feet from me. Ancer Peak hit a wrong note, but kept on playing.

Am I in Jane's kitchen? Am I dancing beside her? *Just who can solve this mystery? Why should it make a fool of me?* No—here I am, outside her window. And I began to laugh, then. With the notion that now I've really gone crazy up here.

Jane laughed, too. She was recalling herself, tying ropes over her little boy to keep him in bed, and furiously feeding him rice. She was remembering her poor little boy, forced to be a pig in the yard. Jane's sorrowful, broken hands filching a book at the doctor's office. Banging down the phone receiver. Scribbling numbers on pads of paper, alone, at midnight. And, I suppose, that because she had already cried about these things, mourned so bitterly, hated herself so keenly, now she could laugh. All of that old self was gone.

That's why I ask the Lord in heaven above—what is this thing called love? Ancer Peak pounded the final few notes hard, angrily.

I see myself, too. In one brilliant, colorless flash. On the back porch steps, my fingers laced, sad because Meg and the bigger kids would not take me along. Then drunk, with blotchy skin, telling George to leave his boyfriend—*"I'd get rid of him."* Getting fucked by David; his dick was too big and it hurt, but I held my breath, clutched a damp pillow. Spent and sweaty, David said he loved me, and I said I loved him, too. I took his picture, then. He protested, put a hand up. In New York City, one spring, I wished the man at a nearby table in a café would look at me. I stared at him. I loved his hair and eyes, his unshaven jaw, the way he sat lazily in his chair. He turned the page of a ragged book and lifted his chin, continued to read. Please look at me, and come to me. He rose, left a bill on the table, glanced in my direction, but I turned my head.

Nobody loved me. On my knees at the foot of my bed. Through bitter, violent sobs. God, if you will please just help me out of this pain, I'll believe in you, I really will believe in you. God, I want to be held, that's what I need, to be touched and loved. God, take away this awful lonely feeling. Exhausted, finally, and tears dried like mud on my cheeks and throat. I lay on my back on the bed. I jerked off. Closed my eyes, heard some people laughing in the hallway. I recognized their voices. They were tripping on acid. Someone said: *It seems like, well, like none of this is even real.* Someone else said: *I know, I know!*

"I'm happy," Jane was saying. "I'm happy, I'm happy." Worn out from her dancing, she stood against the wall, held her arms crossed over her chest and her hands on her shoulders. *What happens now, Jane?* The neatly framed photograph of her mother and sisters had whispered the question to Jane. Jane did not answer.

My hands were against the windowpane, moisture forming a picture of my fingers. Did she know I was out there? Did she know I wanted to come in?

One or two careless notes from Ancer Peak's piano—he could not decide what song to play—and then silence. And then Cindy's high-pitched, anxious bark, which I laughed at. Jane heard it and laughed, too.

Once I left Mark alone for a few minutes. I'd forgotten to bring my film in from the car. I ran out, came right back in. He was in bed, wearing a cotton shirt and a plastic diaper. He looked at me with the richest, most complex, most terrifying expression; excruciating fragility and hunger in those unblinking eyes. Hate, shame, fear. This is how we are when we're dying, I thought. Mark told me if he should live through his illness, he would have to move to another house, because this house would be so full of bad memories. The windows and doors were wide open, for they'd been saying it was the hottest day all year in L.A. A line of amber sweat coursed from his hairline to his mouth, and Mark took the little drop onto his tongue.

"Nothing lasts forever," said my mother.

Jane blew out her candle, watched the band of silver smoke rise straight, curl, disappear. She was thinking of Russell's satiny blue-black hair. She was seeing herself pointing to animal shapes in the clouds, and Russell giggling, squeezing her hand.

Meg dove right in, but I stood at the edge, embarrassed, terrified, hearing angry, impatient voices. I could not jump. I cannot do this. Not into the icy deep, not like this, not here or now, no. God, please help me, please let me dive.

"Hello? Hello, is someone there?"

I eased myself along the side of Jane's house, my palms flat against the wood. I rounded the corner. Jane was on her porch, in the doorway, holding open the screen door. "Hello?" she asked the night.

"Hello," I said.

She turned on the porch light. The pinkish glow barely illumined her. I moved forward, to the steps of Jane's house.

"Hello," she said. "Can I help you?" She sounded severe, like a doctor or a salesclerk or a man on a phone. As anyone would sound who sees a stranger at their porch steps on a cold night like this.

"I don't know, I—"

"Is there something wrong?" Jane asked me. Now she sounded soft. Like your teacher when your lip trembles, you're about to cry, because you're homesick, you do not want to be in school.

"Maybe," was my answer.

She took a step forward. The screen door closed behind her. She brushed a bit of hair away from her eyes. She looked directly at me, gently. But her words were clear, strong. "What is wrong?"

"Maybe—"

"What is wrong?" she asked again.

"Maybe I've never really loved," I said. I looked away from her, down to the crooked stones of the path.

So I was not seeing her, I was only hearing her. Humming some slow tune. Was she thinking, was she deciding who I was and what to say to me? I could not look up. In a second, this was all hilarious and I thought I would burst out laughing, run away, with Cindy at my heels; another second, and I was paralyzed, unfeeling, oblivious of the few drops of rain, a stone statue of Paul, commissioned by Jane. Was she wondering if she ought to bring me in from the rain? Was she afraid of me? No. Jane does not get afraid.

She sighed, deep and satisfied. I listened for the screen door to be opened and closed, for Jane to disappear, leave me here.

"Hello?" I heard.

I looked up at her. Rain pricked my eyelids.

"But who are you? Have we met? Are you from this town?" Jane was standing now with fists on her sides, feet apart, chin slightly raised, as though prepared for some combat, and pleased about it, an amused agitator. My shoulders shrunk, facing this incendiary posture. The rain began falling harder. Cindy moaned. Cindy wanted the warmth of her own home.

My life is made up of all these moments of fragility and hunger— even in sleep, even taking pictures, even laughing, even drunk. With my dick hard as steel, pulsing, and some guy's dick touching my lips or sliding against my throat or pushed into me. Scratching out letters to Meg. At home or away from home. When I think I'm searching, or when I think I've found some shiny, enduring thing.

I wanted to tell Jane that I've taken deep, huge breaths up here. But that they aren't deep or huge enough.

My eyes met her eyes. Our complicity in this story is suddenly apparent, isn't it?

Jane looked so hard, so determined. I was my old breakable self. Jane was possibility. I was merely longing. Paul was the man in the rain, and Jane was the recognition of the man in the rain.

"Do you know me?" Jane asked, as wind whipped the backs of Paul's legs, soaked his trousers. "Do you know me?"

Paul didn't pause or think or wonder. "Yes," said Paul.

FREUD'S BIG
TROUBLE

I

One of the detectives was named Otter. He had a pinkish, tired-looking face. I noticed a collection of mugs with cartoon characters on them lined up on a shelf above his desk—a whimsical sort of thing to collect, but he was in no other way whimsical.

Detective Otter rubbed his eyes with his fingers. "We *want* to believe you," he said. "We're trying, here. You have to understand *our* position."

I said nothing.

"Do you see *our* problem?" asked the other detective, whose name I never learned, and he leaned in closer to me.

Otter continued: "The problem we're faced with here is motivation. Okay?"

"Okay," I said.

"Okay. So, why do you think this little boy would make up such a thing? Why would Christopher just come up with this out of the blue? He says you touched him. You say no, you never touched him. Why would he invent this?"

"I don't know," I answered.

"I mean," Otter went on, "can you think of some kind of motivation for this kid?"

"I don't know," I repeated.

"You don't know," said the other detective, sarcastically.

"I've just been accused of something," I said, looking from one to the other. "That's all I know. You ask if I ever touched the boy—no. What more can I say?" My throat was dry by this time, I needed some water but was afraid to ask.

"See, we have to have a motivation," Otter explained, scratching his hairless head. "I mean it doesn't take Freud to figure out that people don't just do things or say things for no reason at all."

"You don't have to be a Freud," echoed the other detective summarily.

There was a tense silence. The electric clock on the wall hummed.

"Well," I said finally, "well, you know, that was Freud's big trouble."

2

Now I've come to this place called Crossroads Inn. It sits at the middle point of a straight line of highway, in the center of vast flatness, far away from any crossing roads. The property is bordered by a stand of still trees on one side, fields and broken fences on the other. Also, it isn't really an inn. It's a regular motel, an older one, with a dozen identical, connected cabins. You can drive your car right up to your door.

The steady highway noise is almost like ocean waves; after a while you don't notice it anymore, it becomes just loud silence.

My room has a double bed. There's a brown wooden dresser with black handles and a matching desk and chair. There's a shaded lamp with a brass base, casting a muted yellow light across the walls, which are imitation-wood panel. The carpet is gold. The drapes are dark green, heavy; I have them closed. The bathroom is fairly clean, but too bright, with pale green tiles; and two water glasses sit wrapped in paper on the edge of the sink. This place is my home for now. It's small, but it has a cozy feel. I've seen worse. I can even smell the woods— eucalyptus, I think, and pine.

I pulled in just after sunset, having driven all day. I took a shower, then stretched out across the bed, had a drink, smoked a cigarette. Trying to figure out what to do next. I guess from now on I'll spend my nights on motel beds, trying to figure out what to do next.

I had phoned my sister Dorothy from a highway restaurant—I didn't say exactly where I was—and the last thing she said was: "I'll be praying for you. And I hope you'll pray too."

So, I lay there on the bed in this gold-green, dull room. A water glass with scotch was balanced on my chest, rising and falling as I breathed. The ash from the cigarette was getting longer. I thought about praying. But I didn't do it.

The woods. Cabin in the woods. And the smell: damp leaves on the ground. When have I ever been in the woods? When I was a kid, maybe?

The old guy at the motel office who checked me in has some weird throat disease or something, so when he wants to speak he has to push a little microphone into a hole in his throat, and then he sounds like a machine. What people can go through, I was thinking when I saw him. He said the lounge bar across the way stayed open until one A.M.

"Pretty nice place?" I asked.

"It gets lively some nights," he answered in that scratchy, toneless, amplified voice. I think I made a face. But he must be pretty used to people making faces at him.

It was a cool night. I put on a plaid sport shirt, black pants, a jacket. To reach this lounge bar, I had to walk across a wide gravel parking lot, lit by two or three bright flood lamps. My shoes made a crackling sound on the gray pebbles.

The place had an elaborate sign: in red neon script letters it said TRANSFER LOUNGE, above a blue martini glass with the word COCKTAILS winding around the stem, and blinking underneath was ENTERTAINMENT NIGHTLY. I passed through moths frantically circling a bare yellow bulb, pushed the sooty screen door, and walked straight to a bar stool. The bartender was a tiny young man, delicate, with a pretty face. I ordered scotch. The place had a low ceiling, all the lights were red, and there were fake gold chains draped around mirrors on the walls. I was surprised to see quite a few people there, nearly a dozen, sitting at small round tables, laughing, a few at the bar. Right away I felt ready to go back to my room. I didn't like the Transfer Lounge. I stuck two fingers in my drink and licked them. The pretty bartender boy noticed that and frowned.

"Oh, God." A woman had plopped herself on the stool beside me, to my right. I'm uncomfortable when someone is to my right. I have a pretty bad scar over that eyebrow. It's been a problem for me since I was a kid. I'm always conscious of it, trying to hide it. But I can't hide it.

"Oh, God," this woman said again, slapping her knees with the palms of her hands. "You know what's wrong with this place?"

I shook my head.

"I've been here for like half an hour, forty minutes, maybe more like an hour. And the whole time I've been thinking: God, there's something wrong about this place. Just something off, I don't know, *wrong.* Doesn't feel *right.* You ever get that feeling?"

"No," I said. "I never get that."

"Just a feeling? Like something's just wrong? You never get that?"
So I looked right at her eyes. "No."

She glanced away then, but continued talking. "Well, I finally see what the problem is, what just feels so *wrong* in this place. It's music. There's no *music* here. So listen. Can you lend me a quarter for the jukebox?"

The change from my drink was on the bar, wet from the ring the glass had made. I slid a quarter toward her. "Oh, fantastic," she said, "that's great," and she was making her way through the tables toward an old-fashioned jukebox on the other side of the room.

To the bartender I said: "Hey, I thought there was supposed to be entertainment here."

"Well, it all depends on what one considers entertaining," he answered. He was using a fake Hollywood-type English accent.

The woman returned to the seat next to me. "I punched Johnny Mathis. Everyone likes Johnny Mathis."

I stood up then, just casually, holding my drink. I looked around a bit, put my hand in my pocket, took a few steps. And then sat down again on a different stool, on the other side of this woman. So she couldn't see my scar.

"Can I buy you a drink?" I offered.

"Huh? Oh, no. No, I'm A.A. So I really shouldn't. Oh, well, I don't know. Oh, well, all right, maybe just one. How about a screwdriver—"
But before she'd even finished her sentence, the bartender had set the drink before her. "God, thanks," she said to her straw.

She was forty or so. Pretty eyes, green and perfectly round. She had on a dark blue suit, too tight; the shoulders were wide, the skirt went to her knees. The jewelry was cheap. She was carrying a huge black patent-leather handbag, which matched her high heels. Her hair was lifeless, black, cut straight with bangs. Her lipstick was on a little thick, and was an unflattering shade of red. This getup was not a success— anyone would have told her that.

"I work at St. Mary's, the hospital." she said. "I'm a nurse. I'm looking for some kind of apartment or whatever, to share or whatever, but I'm new around here so for right now I'm staying over at the Crossroads. You at the Crossroads?"

I nodded.

"Just check in tonight?"

"That's right."

"It's a funny little place, a little dump kind of, but kind of cute. I'm in 3-B." She got the last of the liquid from the bottom of the glass, practically breathed it through her straw. She rattled her ice.

So I offered: "Can I get you another?"

"Another?" She looked right at me and gave a huge, insincere blink. "Another drink?"

"Oh, right. You're A.A. I forgot you were A.A."

"What's your name?" she asked.

"Jack."

"Jack, I'm Ida. Jack, I've really had some problems with drinking. That's the thing. I mean, it's a long story. And so then I went into A.A. and stopped drinking for a while. But then I started again. Then I stopped again. See, I mean, really, it *is* a long story. So, an hour ago I was A.A., I wasn't drinking. But now . . . well, now I'm drinking again. Do you see what I mean?"

"I think so, Ida."

"What I mean is: it doesn't really make any difference."

"Yes, I see."

"So, I'd really *love* another drink. And why don't I buy this round?" She was smiling at me. Her lipstick was caked and cracking at the corners of her mouth. Those huge eyes were very charming, very sweet, friendly. I liked Ida.

We talked about her mostly, but she was a constantly changing subject; every bit of information was revised after a moment or two, every revelation amended. "Well, the truth is," she admitted, "I'm not exactly a nurse. That's what I want to be, that's what I'm planning on. Right now I'm in the radiology lab, X rays. Which is fine, you know, it's fine." Later, after another drink: "Well, actually . . . I've been sort of an assistant in radiology for three months. They laid me off, though. See, they're laying off tons of people, and I hadn't been with them too long. You know how it goes."

All of Ida's story went this way: circular, spiraling from some wish point down to some truth point. She was married; well, not married but living with a guy, engaged; well, she *had* been living with him. And he was a doctor—no, he was in medical school—no, he worked at the hospital.

She was not really drunk. She would sip slowly, noisily, and then order another before she'd even finished what she had. At first she had asked me for a cigarette; then she began pointing to my package and lifting her eyebrows; finally, she simply helped herself.

I'd said very little. After a half hour or so, I rose to leave. She, still seated, was surprised by my movement. "You going?" she asked.

"Kind of tired, Ida. Nice meeting you."

"Well, listen, well, hey," Ida said, grabbing her purse and keys, flustered, "listen, I'll walk back with you. Don't want to end up walking through that parking lot alone, you know. It's late and everything."

But I was already at the door; I held it open for her, and she ducked under my arm, scooted outside, laughing. "Well, night-night, children," said the pretty-boy bartender with his phony English accent, smiling at me, winking. I wanted to punch his face, then. He's lucky I didn't punch his face.

I kept a few steps in front of Ida as we made our way back across the gravel. Ahead, the tiny cabins were mostly dark, and framed by silhouettes of tall trees against the gray night sky.

"You know this whole abortion business?" Ida was saying. "I've had two abortions. And I mean, God, I'm so happy I had them. Really, I mean God, can you imagine me with a kid?" She stumbled, but did not fall, and she laughed. "Everyone gets so emotional about all this stuff, abortion and all this stuff. Like the rights of animals. Like kids on drugs. Like people having guns. I don't care anything about abortions or animals or kids or drugs or guns or anything." Ida laughed, an unpleasant, squawking sound.

My cabin was I-B. I walked straight to it, intent on going inside, unwilling to have any more talk. Ida's was two doors down. Her car was parked in front of her room: a gray Buick with giant rust spots forming a pattern across the hood, like a map of the world. I was not looking at Ida, but I could feel her there, sense her hesitating with her key, watching me. Without turning, my eyes on the doorknob, I said: "Good night," and after I had closed my door I heard her call: "Hey, yeah, good night."

I had a beautiful, peaceful dream. I was walking in a forest. I was out of breath, because I'd made my way up a steep incline and reached the top. And I paused before making my descent. I looked all around. The floor of the forest was chocolate brown, the trees black, dotted with bits of vivid green. I was serene. I leaned against a tree and put my palm on a thick branch, rubbed the coarse bark. I rubbed hard, harder, until the skin of my hand and fingers was bright red and stinging; but I did not feel pain.

I woke suddenly, sat straight up, as though this dream had been some kind of a nightmare. But it was a lovely dream, soft and sweet. I can't explain why I was so terrified.

My clock said two A.M. I lighted a cigarette, pushed my hair back with my fingers.

"Hey, hello?" It was Ida outside my door, and the way she spoke made me think she'd been there for some time. "Hey, are you awake in there?" she stage-whispered.

I slid out of the bed, turned on the table lamp. I was naked and moved to throw my coat over myself, or the blanket. But, then I didn't. I walked to the door and opened it halfway and stood so she could see me.

"What is it you want, Ida?"

"Oh, oh God, you were asleep?" She stared directly at my chin, avoiding my eyes, avoiding every part of my exposed body. I guess I was enjoying her discomfort.

"I was asleep, yes."

"Oh. Oh, well . . ." She was wearing a pale blue quilted robe, quite worn, and her high heels and was hugging a motel ice bucket to her chest. "I couldn't get to sleep. So then I thought . . . I don't know. I brought some Cokes," she said, and lifted the lid of the bucket to show me the cans.

I did not reply.

She turned slightly, gazed at the brown woven rug in front of my door. "I guess if you're . . . I mean, if you're . . ."

Still I said nothing. I can't say I either wanted her to go or wished to invite her in. I didn't care about Ida. She was just there.

Abruptly, she faced me; she looked at my eyes. "Mister," she said. "I need a friend." Her expression then was suddenly sober, departing from the frivolous, inconsistent impression she had made earlier that night. Now she was serious about something. And she did not even wait for me to answer. She slid past me, into my room—invited by herself, by her own need. And I was just there.

4

Men are for sex. Men are things. They are jawlines and muscular necks, firm shoulders, broad chests, round, tough butts, strong legs. They are faces—an intelligent brow; pretty, moist, thick lips; ears too big or too small; cheeks too soft or too chiseled. Men are dicks.

That's how I see men: as though I'm scrutinizing fruit at the market or appreciating statues in a museum—I like what I like, don't really notice the rest. It's how most men see women, I guess. And women, for me . . . women are real people. Men are things; women are people. That's it.

Ida kicked off her slippers and sat cross-legged in the cheap arm-chair, in front of the window. I slipped on my trousers and a sweater. I sat on the edge of the bed. "See, I'm in trouble," she began. "I'm in big trouble. See, I wasn't just laid off at the hospital. I was fired."

"I have a bottle of scotch. You want some?"

Ida shook her head. Then: "Maybe I'd better."

I rose, rinsed out the glasses, poured us each a drink. "They gave me all kinds of warnings," she went on. "They even had me seeing this counselor woman. And, then, of course, I was going to my A.A."

The thick, dark green drapes were not fully closed. Behind Ida and a bit to the right, I saw a small pickup truck turn into the drive and pull into the space beside my car. Its headlights sent a strip of white over the carpet, up and across the wall.

Ida had her head down, staring into her drink. "So I was doing pretty good. I really was. I hadn't had a drink in six weeks. And then there was this one patient, this Mrs. Russo. Bitchy old broad. She fell in her bathroom or something, broke her hip."

I could see the driver's side of the truck. The door opened. A muscular man wearing a cowboy hat had stepped out. He wore boots, too, and a bandana knotted around his neck. He reached inside the truck and grabbed a canvas bag, tossed the strap over one shoulder. The passenger-side door, out of my sight, opened and slammed. The cowboy said something, then laughed. Another man—thinner, a bit younger—walked slowly around behind the truck, also carrying a bag, also wearing a hat. He slapped his cowboy friend on the back.

Ida sniffled. "Mrs. Russo, she's the one who started it all. She told Calvin, who's in charge of radiology during my shift, all these complaints about me. Oh, she said she thought I was drunk, that she could smell alcohol on my breath and everything. So, naturally, I mean, Calvin had to go to Dr. Strauss, who's like the head of everything. Then they brought me into the office."

The cowboys went into the room between Ida's and mine. When their door closed, my walls trembled. I had to stand up, suddenly. I had to walk over to the wall that separated our two rooms. I touched the wall. I felt chilled then, so I grabbed the thin blanket from the bed and wrapped it around myself. I took my seat again.

"Can I?" wondered Ida, plaintively extending her empty glass. I nodded and she poured more from the bottle. "Well, so anyway, they brought me in and asked me all these questions. This cunt Mrs. Russo said that I was irresponsible. She said I'd been giggling and stuff. She said I'd messed up the first pictures and had had to make her sit for another set and everything. I don't know. And Calvin was there looking really serious, Dr. Strauss was looking mean. He asked me, like, Okay, what do you have to say for yourself?"

A laugh from one of the cowboys, the younger one I think. Then their T.V. was turned on.

Ida shifted in her chair noisily. "So I said, Listen. I said, Listen, it's not true. Strauss said, 'Well, Calvin has told me you've had these problems with alcohol.' And I said, 'I know, I *know* that. But not anymore. I'm doing really good now. Six weeks.' Strauss said, 'Well,

Mrs. Russo smelled alcohol on your breath.' I said—and I was really kind of frantic, I stood up—'No, no, she *couldn't* have smelled alcohol. I *hadn't* been drinking.' "

Ida sipped her scotch now, breathing heavily, her expression furious. We said nothing for some moments. I could hear trucks passing on the highway. The T.V. next door was turned off. "Then what happened?" I asked.

"Then?" She was a bit drunk now, I guess; her words were indistinct, her dry lips formed into a frown, her eyes settled nowhere particularly. "Oh, then they tried to calm me down and everything. Finally they said, 'Well, okay, we'll give you a urine test and see what the results are.' So I said, '*Great,* that would be *great,*' because I thought that would clear me." She waved her right arm in a broad sweep, then brought it close to her, across her chest, the fingers on her shoulder. Mumbling now: "And, but, well, they gave me the test and the test came up positive for alcohol. I couldn't believe it. I told them, I said it must be some kind of weird mistake or something. Or whatever. I just couldn't believe it. I was railroaded. Framed or something. I mean, I was innocent. I am innocent."

5

The closest town is twelve miles up the highway. There's a funny little boardwalk there, made to look like the Old West, with a saloon and wagon wheels, an Indian crafts store and vendors. In the morning, Ida and I took my car there and went for a stroll. Newspapers and reddish dead leaves were swept up by the wind, encircled our feet. A restaurant called Junior's has picnic tables set up outside, under a tin roof. We ordered Cokes and hamburgers.

"Pretty dull little town, isn't it?" Ida asked. She had a white scarf over her hair and because of the breeze, she held a hand on her head to keep it in place. She wore enormous sunglasses, and silver hoop earrings that looked more like hardware than jewelry. "You know, Jack, I'm feeling a lot better now. Thanks for that talk last night. I was pretty smashed, I know." She laughed, and a dab of mustard fell from her mouth to her chin, and she laughed again as she wiped it off. "Oh, God, things look different in the morning. Don't they?"

"Everything always looks the same to me," I replied.

"There's an A.A. meeting tonight. Eight o'clock. At the Unitarian church. I'm going."

I could see a truck approaching, moving slowly down the main street; in a moment I was sure it was the cowboys' truck. It sped up, spinning its wheels loudly, and when it disappeared a cloud of rose-colored dust was left suspended.

"Maniacs," said Ida, popping the last bite of her hamburger into her mouth, then rubbing her fingers together. "You know," she said, leaning toward me, "I've told you my trouble. So, what's your trouble?"

"How do you know I have any trouble?"

She smiled slyly. "Oh, you're in trouble too, Jack."

I picked up the grease-stained bill for our meal, looked it over.

She sat straight. "Oh. I don't want to pry or anything."

"I'm not much of a talker, Ida," I said, not looking at her.

"Well, that's fine. Really. You don't have to talk at all, Jack." I thought she was being sincere about this. By now I knew Ida was a confessor type, that she had a need to reveal herself. She wanted me to know her. Some people are like that. But I did not sense she was asking for payment in kind. She stood, straightened her sunglasses, tugged at her scarf, arranged her purse, and smiled—a very warm, if deliberate smile. "Come on, Jack. Let's go home."

6

After hours in that cluttered, stuffy office, Otter finally asked me: "You *are* homosexual, isn't that right? Or gay, or whatever you want to call it?"

"Well, yes," I said.

And the other detective sort of sniffed and said: "I mean, we really have to face up to that fact."

I said: "Oh, well, I think I've faced up to that."

7

Now it seems the cowboys have checked out. I wish we could have met. I wish they had slapped me on the back and told me jokes. I wish that they had told me, Go ahead, hop on in our truck, and that we'd all gone away together.

Ida is off at her A.A. meeting. I've been reading through my clippings. I've read them dozens of times. Naturally, the entire episode is painful to me—I hold my breath when I read the report and the quotes.

But I am most affected by the description of me: the age, height, hair color, eye color, and thin scar above the right eyebrow. That scar. Something I've been trying to conceal my whole life—there it is, printed in the newspaper.

When I pull the clippings from their envelope I always wonder if I shouldn't just burn them now. I wonder why I'm carrying them around, what they mean, what use they are. But I'm not ready to get rid of them. I must need them. Maybe I should see a psychiatrist.

Sleep. Not a dream really. More like memories, real memories, but unlocated, uncontrollable. That family, standing in my driveway. That crazy mother in front, the dull father behind her, the little boy, Christopher, holding her hand. Their pale, severe faces. The father's worried, the mother's furious. Christopher's face—can't make that out. "I don't know *what* you're talking about," I say. "I don't know what you're *talking* about!" I am shouting at his mother and father, looking from one to the other.

Finally, I take one step down from my porch. The family takes a step back.

Now, directly to Christopher: "Have you told your parents these things?" No eyes, just the top of his head, messy copper-colored hair. Beautiful hair. Mother pulls him closer to her, hard, and puts an arm around his chest. She's yelling something; the father is speaking low, holding up both hands flat, to calm, to be reasonable.

To Christopher: "Christopher, you know this is not true. Why have you told your parents this? You know it is not true. Christopher?" I question sternly. His head is still and lowered, but the eyes look up, the brows lift. He bites his bottom lip, to keep from crying.

Oh, no, don't cry, Christopher.

I came out of this half-sleep exhausted, frowning. I went into the bathroom and splashed cold water on my face. I dried with one of those thin, white towels and barely glanced at my reflection in the mirror. I've been afraid of mirrors lately. I look only long enough to push my hair into place.

I heard the sound of a motor outside my room. It was not the cowboys, returning for me. It was Ida, pulling into her spot sloppily and fast. I drew back a corner of the drape. She took some time assembling herself, getting out of the car, locking the door; then it seemed she'd forgotten something, so she unlocked the car, searched the seat and floor. Whatever she'd lost she decided was unimportant; her whole body, her movement was a magnificent shrug of dismissal. I watched her walk unsteadily across the parking lot, could hear her heels on the gravel. Her figure was illuminated in spots as she passed beneath the buzzing floodlamps. She reached the Transfer Lounge, pushed the screen door, sent the moths scattering, walked right in.

8

This morning I decided to leave, to keep going. I drove to town for gas and maps, then came back to the Crossroads to check out and gather my things. Today was overcast, misty. "Looks like rain," I told that guy at the desk.

"Been a drought lately," he answered, the device against his throat. Then he coughed, and he had not removed the microphone, so the cough was amplified. It sounded like a toy engine. I laughed.

I approached I-B and saw my door was open. I thought the maid must be there already. As I stepped to the doorway, there was Ida, standing on the other side of my room, by the desk. She turned around quickly, breathed in as though startled. But she was smiling.

"Morning, Ida," I said, and proceeded inside. My bag was on the bed. I undid its straps and opened it out flat, to begin packing.

"Morning, Jack," she said.

I didn't look at her, just went about tossing shirts and pants into the bag. I asked how her A.A. meeting had gone. She said: "Oh, just fine." I asked what she was planning for the day. "Oh, nothing much." She sounded like a kid, dying to tell a secret, playing games.

I snapped shut my case. I turned to look at Ida. She had her hands in front of her, holding the straps of that huge, ridiculous purse. Her dress was cut tight, framed by ruffles at the sleeves and hem, cream-colored with red polka dots. She was smiling and rocking very slightly from side to side.

"Heading out, Jack?"

"Seems that way."

"Well, it was fun meeting you, Jack."

"You too, Ida."

"Now I know your trouble, Jack."

"Is that so?"

"That's right. And your name isn't even Jack."

I put my hands in my pockets and leaned against the open door. "Well?"

"You were accused of something. I wasn't even meaning to snoop or anything. I mean, I *wanted* to, but I didn't set *out* to. You know? Anyway, I opened that drawer." She pointed vaguely toward the desk. "I wanted some stationery."

"Writing a letter to someone, Ida?"

"And saw those clippings you have in there. So, now I guess I know it all. You were accused of fiddling with a little neighbor boy. Everyone thinks you did it, and so you ran away."

"Well, if I hadn't run away over that, I'd probably have run away over something else."

"That's funny, Jack. That's probably true, too. You're a very honest person, Jack. So?"

"So?" I repeated.

Ida moved leisurely to the armchair, seated herself, crossed her legs. "Ten-year-old boy. Lived right next door to you. That's quite a story."

"You know how the newspapers are." Now I moved too, and settled myself across the bed, up on one elbow.

She leaned forward. "So, did you do it?"

"Does it matter?"

"No."

"Why do you care, Ida?"

"I don't care. I truly don't. People do all kinds of things. And people don't do all kinds of things."

"It just doesn't matter to you?"

"Can't you tell by now?" she asked, straightening in her seat. "Nothing matters to me."

"Well, what if I say I didn't do it?"

"I'd say I didn't think you did."

"And what if I say I did do it?"

"I'd say, oh . . . well . . . I thought so."

9

Now, the road. Gorgeous, aimless. A straight double yellow line, with no divergence, no subtlety. I'll take this road, but eventually I will probably turn around and take it back again. I passed a filling station and a few yards from it a woman was set up at a card table with a painted sign reading: PSYCHIC, $7.00—KNOW YOUR FUTURE. And I thought about stopping, I even slowed down. But I can't see wasting seven bucks—I already know my future. It is now, this road. It is that kitten just ahead, squashed by a car, splayed across the yellow lines in bloody pieces. It is the rows of corn, battered by the strong, dusty wind. It is faded ads for soft drinks and cigarettes on these dying barns.

I did pull off the road some miles back to look at my map. I was thinking, Well, sooner or later, I have to face my trouble. And suddenly a man and woman were standing at my car, leaning down, peering in the window at me. I was startled. They were very old, with yellowish, leathery skin. "You in any trouble?" the man asked, and the woman smiled. I had to laugh. But I was angry, too. I pressed hard on the gas; the tires squealed. I could see those old people in my mirror, watching after me, shaking their heads, so shocked at how things are, how the world is. Shocked, I guess, at how much life has changed since their day.

THIS IS NOT
THAT

I

It was a morning in early spring. It had rained, so muddy puddles had formed at the curbs; the piles of fallen leaves had been soaked until they were purple-black; water dripped from the tin gutters of the houses. The sky was gray with patches of silver brightness where the sun was beginning to burn through.

Mrs. Weddings awoke at dawn crying and could not figure why, could not get back to sleep. She put on her comfortable yellow housecoat. She pulled up and pinned her long, graying hair. She despised her hair.

She did not know why, but she wished somehow to continue crying, so she leaned her elbows on her dresser, scrutinized the old photographs flattened under its glass top. Pictures of her younger self, her family, all the cars they'd had over the years. Her husband had loved taking pictures of the cars. The vacations, the birthdays. Celeste at ten riding in a horse show. Francis at thirteen in a school play.

But it all left Mrs. Weddings a bit cold; her eyes remained dry, and she was surprised that this assembled portrait of her lovely past did not excite a stronger, more desperate mourning. She walked downstairs to the kitchen, sat at the table by the window, and smoked a cigarette, sipped a too-milky cup of coffee.

As always, around nine, Celeste knocked on the wooden part of the back screen door and called: "Yoo-hoo, yoo-hoo," and came on in. "Morning, Mother."

"Morning, Celeste."

Celeste set her briefcase on the kitchen table. She was a social worker for the county. She began unpacking a bag of tomatoes and fruit she'd brought. "Good tomatoes, Mother. Peaches aren't ripe yet, though. Have you been up long?"

Mrs. Weddings lied and said no.

"Did you hear about the little Kennedy boy? Brain disease." Celeste poured herself a mug of coffee. "Eileen Westerhauser told me. Tumor. Progressive kind of thing." She leaned her hip against the counter, blew on the coffee, and sipped. Celeste always spoke in short, chopped sentences and phrases. She bent her knees, leaned forward to check her reflection in the side of the toaster. "Terrible thing. You know, don't you, those Kennedys are relatives of the real Kennedys."

"Yes, I heard something like that."

"Distant cousins."

Celeste loved the morning talk shows—"You should watch them, Mother. Real informative"—all about transplants, husbands cheating on their wives, sex changes, artificial limbs, gruesome diseases. Now Celeste moved about the kitchen, aimlessly tidying, talking in that rapid, uncaring way of hers about a transsexual who wanted to get pregnant, and she did not look once at her mother.

But Mrs. Weddings was watching Celeste. Really, why does she wear those brown-and-beige outfits all the time, all the time, and the hair is so plain and dull, really. Celeste could be a pretty woman but she makes herself appear so hard, she talks so fast and hard. She makes herself seem just mean and phony. All that brown and beige, so unappealing, and then she has on that ridiculous bright blue scarf at her neck and blue shadow on her eyes, really, she has such bad taste.

Mrs. Weddings certainly never thought her daughter would grow up to have such bad taste.

Celeste was saying: "So I said, Well, fine, we'll *go* to Maine this summer. No point to arguing. I said, Someone's got to give in here. You want to go to Maine so much, we'll go to Maine, I said, and that's that."

Oh, how she bickers with that husband, Mrs. Weddings reflected. And Celeste always sacrifices, always is generous and compromising and clear-thinking, and then she fumes with resentment. She used to be that way with Francis, too. Celeste likes to be the good girl, always has. Celeste has been fuming her whole life.

Celeste did not really smoke as a habit, but she liked sometimes to take puffs of her mother's cigarettes; now she blew thin, quick cones of smoke and was talking about someone Mrs. Weddings did not know. "She's a hypocrite if you ask me. I happen to know personally that she had two abortions when we were in high school. *High school.* And now she's making this *big* stink about her daughter being pregnant. Anyway, Mother, I'm running late."

Celeste stood now half inside the back doorway, holding the screen door against her shoulder. "Anything you need?"

"No, Celeste, no thank you, dear."

"What are you going to do today?"

Every morning Celeste asked this question and it sent a shudder of panic through Mrs. Weddings, for now she had to think quickly: what *would* she do?

"I have some letters to write, a little shopping to do," the mother said miserably.

"Well, that's fine, Mother," and Celeste was gone. The door of her car slammed, the car started, sped away. Celeste was always in a hurry.

Mrs. Weddings rose, poured more coffee into her cup. "Those atrocious brown shoes," she said aloud. "How can Celeste wear those atrocious shoes?"

II

By noon, when the whistle at the fire station sounded, the sun had finally reached through the week's dismal haze, like a fast explosion of bright white; the lawns were hard and brown; the houses of the town were washed copper.

Mrs. Weddings sat at her front window. She had a book open on her lap, an old mystery she'd read before. She saw a little neighbor boy was drawing with chalk on the uneven sidewalk in front of his house; that rumpled Mr. Simms came down the road on his bicycle; the ancient, peevish dog from Pell's Hardware lumbered across her yard, sniffed her flowers. Her white curtain was drawn to the side and a breeze swelled into the room, touched her shoulder, then was pulled out, like an inhale and an exhale, Mrs. Weddings thought, like a deep sigh.

She sat quite content, watching the dreary progress of the neighborhood, and it was some seconds before she realized there was someone on her front porch. She moved quickly and opened the door. "Who's there?"

"Hello, Mother."

Mrs. Weddings said nothing. She knew the figure and voice and she was not really surprised.

"I have to come in. I'm tired. I have to lie down."

Mrs. Weddings stood still, was silent, and after a moment her son walked past her, into the house and up the front stairs, carrying a red plaid suitcase which Mrs. Weddings remembered so well.

Mrs. Weddings prepared a glass of iced tea and a plate with apple sections and pieces of cheese, put this all on a tray, and walked up the stairs. "Francis?" she said, [ ]ng his door with two fingers. "Francis, I've got a little snack here. [ ] pushed open the door.

Her son was stretched o[ ] the bed, eyes closed; his hands were behind his head and his skin[ ] rms and sharp elbows seemed unconnected to him, projecting aw[ ] rdly. Mrs. Weddings set the tray on the bureau and stood lookin[ ] own at him, her arms folded. "You don't look good, Francis."

He did not open his eyes. [ ]n not good, Mother."

"Well, have you *been* to the [ ]ctor?"

"Like Catholics go to chur[ ]

"And what does he say?"

"She."

"All right, whatever, she the[ ] What does she say?"

Francis breathed in deeply a[ ] turned on his side. "She says what they all say all the time."

Mrs. Weddings, agitated, too[ ] slim, bent pack of cigarettes from the pocket of her yellow housec[ ] removed one and smoothed it out, lit it. "Here we go all around it a[ ]n. You can't just tell me what they say?"

Francis sat up abruptly, cross[ ] his legs, and pointed to the tray. "Okay, let's have the iced tea."

Mrs. Weddings handed him the glass and he took several full swallows. "Well, I'm anemic. I have several really repulsive fungal infections. My T cells are around a hundred, my P-24 is five ninety, my white blood cell count is below fifteen hundred."

"Wait, wait, wait," said his mother, "just hold the phone, mister."

Francis laughed. Mrs. Weddings sat on the edge of his bed and tapped cigarette ash into her cupped palm. "Explain T cells and these other things."

"Mother, I'm very tired. Is that apple?"

"Yes, and there's a little cheese."

"I'll wait, I'm not hungry."

"I want to know what all these numbers you're telling me are," Mrs. Weddings demanded.

"I don't even know myself, Mother, really. I can tell you everything's abnormal, everything's bad. That's all I know." Francis turned onto his front now, folded his hands together under his chest. He closed his eyes.

Mrs. Weddings set the half-finished glass of iced tea back on the tray. She decided she'd leave the apple and cheese. She decided she'd make some potato pancakes and cranberry sauce, something light for supper. She decided she'd run down and get some ice cream. Francis always used to love ice cream.

He wasn't only thin. He was drawn, ghostly. His eyes were huge, circled by shadow; his cheekbones were like hard little balls attached to his face. His hair was wispy, his ears stuck out. How was her daughter so big and healthy and dull and her son so sickly, weak, but so funny and smart? Mrs. Weddings had always wondered about this—even before Francis got sick—about the differences of her children. How was it Francis was so sneaky and dramatic, disappearing sometimes, for years sometimes, while Celeste was so reliable and solid and predictable? Celeste always took care of things, followed through, did what she said she'd do. Celeste always had to be the good girl. But, Mrs. Weddings could *talk* to her son. She slid the afghan over him and very quietly left the room.

She prepared supper and set the table beautifully, but Francis didn't feel like eating. He came downstairs in his bulky white robe and they sat before the fire with mugs of hot chocolate and cigarettes.

"Look at all these pills I have to take," he said, and emptied seven or eight bottles from a wrinkled paper bag onto the rug. "These are sleeping pills, these are for depression, these are for the horrible cramps I've been getting in my legs—"

"What cramps, what do you mean cramps?" his mother wanted to know.

"Cramps, Mother. Cramps, I don't know what kind. Then these are antivirals and these are antihistamines. I'm like a pharmacy or something."

Mrs. Weddings pushed back a stray bit of hair with her wrist, looked away.

"Oh, I'm just pooped," Francis said. "I'll just barely make it up to my room." But he only pushed out his reed-thin legs on the sofa so that the bottoms of his feet pressed against his mother's knee, and there he fell asleep.

Mrs. Weddings found she could not remember much about Francis as a child. He always was a genius, he always said amusing things, astonishing things. Adults were fascinated with him, children were rather distant. He had been very private and secretive when he was young; it was as though he were holding on, gritting his teeth until he could grow up.

She really came to adore Francis when he was out of college. He graduated early, at only nineteen years old, and he went to live in the city. He would come home to visit, always unannounced, and he did cause some trouble. He drank too much. He argued with his father, he needed money frequently. Sometimes he'd bring a boyfriend home— these were handsome, brawny, ignorant men, usually with no money. His father complained that they were very common, which made Francis laugh. Things got broken, even stolen. Cars got dented. His father brooded and called Francis careless, wasteful, thoughtless. After a week or so, Francis would leave hastily, angrily; and it would be a long silence, passing holidays, passing changes in the town, in the seasons, in the faces of his parents. They even had a hard time tracking Francis down when his father died, and Celeste had been bitter about that ever since.

Francis is always trouble, too smart, he acts too superior, does whatever he pleases—this was what had been said of Francis Weddings from his earliest days, by all the family, by his father especially. Even so, Mrs. Weddings saw some kind aspect to this queer boy. She saw it now as he slept and the dying fire painted his pale face gold. Francis really did know how to live. Even as she worried for her son, she felt a sweet, painless envy. For his expansiveness of spirit, his prosperous nature that could never be concealed or confined by a little house in a little town.

"He practically terrorizes you, Mother," Celeste declared the next morning. "We all know this isn't the best place for him in his condition, but he just waltzes right in, and you let it happen."

Mrs. Weddings sighed and turned the radio on, moved the dial to the station that played those fabulous old big band records. She simply could not talk to Celeste.

"Anyway," continued Celeste, too loudly, dragging from her mother's cigarette and smearing its end with the most ordinary shade of red lipstick, "before I left the house this morning I was watching my show and they had on these teenage Satanists. Incredible, Mother, what these kids are up to. Ritual animal murders. Sacrifices."

Celeste took a dishcloth from its rack by the sink, dampened it, and swept circles across the counter. Mrs. Weddings, watching Celeste's behind, thought her daughter was putting on some weight. Today she was dressed in a tan tailored suit, slightly too small, with navy-blue pumps. Navy-blue pumps with a tan suit—how *did* her daughter ever get like this? And an impossible fake-gold bird brooch at her collar—hideous.

Rather furiously wiping the faucet now, Celeste asked: "Will Francis be down before I have to leave?"

"Here I am," came his voice from the doorway.

"Morning, Francis," said Mrs. Weddings.

Celeste turned around. She pulled the wet rag to her breast and all but gasped.

"My God, Celeste," her brother said, "you look like an airline stewardess."

That's *just* what I was thinking, thought Mrs. Weddings.

His sister took a step forward. "Francis, how are you feeling?"

He seated his thin frame on a cushion on the kitchen chair. "I don't feel too ill, really. I feel . . . sad, I think."

No one knew what to say.

Mrs. Weddings rose and poured him coffee.

The three sat for some time. Francis asked after Celeste's husband, about her job with the county, about her new car. "And you're taking good care of Mother?"

"I stop by every morning, don't I, Mother?"

"Every morning, every single morning."

Celeste was suddenly and inexplicably moved to prepare a bowl of tuna fish: she mixed in some mayonnaise and a dollop of mustard, cut up some onions for it, wrapped the bowl, and put it in the refrigerator. "Now, there's lunch for you two," said she triumphantly.

Francis whispered to his mother: "What about dessert?"

"And now I'm running late," Celeste said, taking her briefcase and heading toward the door. She did not ask about her mother's plans for the day. She asked her brother: "So, Francis, how long do you think you'll be here?"

"I haven't quite figured that out yet. I don't know."

"Well, then. I'm sure we'll see each other again," and she was out the door and into her new car and driving jerkily but with great purpose down their street.

IV

Weeks passed. It was summer and raining lightly in the mornings, then clearing up by noon. There were frequent soft breezes, which carried the scents of all the gardens through the neighborhood.

Francis had had some books sent to him, and spent his afternoons on the porch reading and occasionally drifting off to sleep. He read James M. Cain's *The Postman Always Rings Twice;* Orwell's *Nineteen Eighty-Four;* a biography of Frances Farmer and another of Zelda Fitzgerald; Forster's *A Passage to India;* several novels by the Victorian women authors he adored; James Thurber short stories; and a true account of a mass murderer, which he thought Celeste would probably also enjoy.

Mrs. Weddings and her son ate small, uncomplicated meals. They sat at the kitchen table and talked and listened to the big band show. In the evenings, if it was not too cold, they went to the front porch and, lit by the orange bulb, sipped brandy and looked across the road, into the neighbor's lighted windows.

Francis said: "Celeste watches those silly television shows. You can get more intrigue and excitement looking in other people's windows. As crazy things happen right on your own street as they ever do on television."

"Are you feeling well, Francis? Do you need a blanket?"

"You seem to think blankets are a cure for everything, Mother."

"Don't make fun of me, don't fuss with me."

Francis passed a finger over his lower lip, blinked slowly, distantly. "No, I don't mean to. I'm sorry. I have a silly feeling, it's the brandy."

"I go through enough with your sister," said Mrs. Weddings, pouting.

She lit a cigarette and tossed the match into a potted geranium. "What will happen, Francis? I'm serious now. What do you think is going to happen?"

"I don't know."

"That's funny," she answered quickly, "because you always used to know everything."

"That's true. These days, I guess I don't know much of anything. I mean, all right, not to be coy about this whole thing. It looks like I might die. And so I came up here."

Francis' father used to say that Francis always brought his trouble right to their doorstep. When things got bad for him—debts, men, drinking—Francis would pack it all in that red plaid suitcase and ring their bell.

"I came up here to get some good old-fashioned sympathy," said Francis, and his mother said: "That isn't funny."

"No, no, I know."

"Because you won't get any sympathy from *me*," said his mother sternly.

"Yes, I will." Francis pushed himself up slowly so that he was resting on his elbows. He leaned his head back. "All right, this is my favorite Shakespeare. A sonnet. 'Let me not to the marriage of true minds / Admit impediments.' " He repeated the line. "Now listen, closely. All right. 'Love is not love / Which alters when it alteration finds, / Or bends with the remover to remove.' Blah blah blah—" Francis waved his hand, but his mother, anyway, was not paying much attention. "And then it goes: 'Love's not Time's fool, though rosy lips and cheeks / Within his bending sickle's compass come—' "

" 'Sickle's compass'?" puzzled Mrs. Weddings.

" 'Love alters not with his brief hours and weeks, / But bears it out even to the edge of doom.' "

"I think," Mrs. Weddings said, and she was feeling the brandy a bit, "I think Celetts—"

Francis laughed. "You mean Celeste?"

His mother laughed, put the tips of her fingers to her lips. "Ce-leste . . . I think she likes to look at queer people because she's so ordinary herself. You know? She gets excited by all these freakish types of people. And I think she—in a way—really envies them some."

"I think we should get off to bed."

"But, do you think I'm right? I mean, you did study all about psychology and things. What do you think?"

"I think you're getting drunk and if you topple over or something, I can't carry you. I think you'd better get up to bed."

They laughed about Celeste, but it was not mean; and they laughed watching that rotten old dog from Pell's Hardware poop on someone's front porch and then slink away. She kissed her son's forehead, and even that made them both laugh.

Climbing the stairs Mrs. Weddings realized something terribly important and she rushed to her room to write it down. On the back of the receipt from the pharmacy where she had been that afternoon to pick up her son's pills, she wrote:

My boy Francis—maybe there's nothing to be especially proud of in him. But he's a delightful person, and that's a rare thing. He's a happy person, despite so much bad. And whatever he ever needs to do is all right with me. I take Francis just the way he is. Period.

She folded this paper and put it under the glass top of her dresser.

Mrs. Weddings finally decided, with Francis' encouragement, to have her long gray hair cut, and while she was at it, took a rinse and a dye. Now, it was close to her head and chocolate-colored.

She came home one afternoon with a book of wallpaper samples. This was the kind of thing Francis loved to help with, at which he could be so fun and dear. When she walked in, though, he was on the sofa in the front room, bent over, struggling with short, uneven breaths. Her white curtain blew across him.

"What is it? Francis, what is it?"

He did not speak.

Mrs. Weddings was growing frantic. "Pills? You need some kind of pill, Francis? Which one, talk to me." After one second of silence, she turned, ran into the kitchen, and phoned for an ambulance. She phoned Celeste, too, and arranged that they meet at the hospital.

Celeste flap-flapped her sandals pacing the hospital waiting room. She was wearing faded lime-green pants which came just to her ankles, and an ill-fitting red sweater. She looked like a Christmas ornament, Mrs. Weddings observed sadly. That husband of hers sat in a corner, flipping through a magazine, coughing and waving his hand to indicate without subtlety that he objected to Mrs. Weddings' cigarette fumes.

After midnight, a young man doctor, Dr. Silverstein, and an older woman nurse, also named Silverstein, came to speak with the family. Francis had pneumocystis carinii, the family were told, a problematical form of pneumonia associated with AIDS; it looked under control, however. Francis also seemed to have several lesions on his legs which might indicate Kaposi's sarcoma, a cancer associated with AIDS. Dr. Silverstein recommended that Francis rest there for a few days and then return to the city, where he could be examined by his regular doctor.

"Is his regular doctor named Silverstein too?" Mrs. Weddings asked softly. It was supposed to be sort of a joke.

"Why, no," the nurse answered, puzzled.

Mrs. Weddings visited daily, brought flowers and a deck of cards, smuggled in cigarettes for her son. Within the week, he was discharged. Francis accepted Celeste's offer to drive him down to the city, for he did not wish to make the train ride alone: he was still weak.

Celeste had late meetings at her social-work job and she did not pull her car into Mrs. Weddings' driveway until early evening. She apologized for her lateness and put Francis' bag in the trunk.

Mrs. Weddings stayed on the porch, leaning her hip into the railing. She kept her arms folded across her chest, held a cigarette. Francis joined her and brought a small inhaler from his jacket pocket, sucked on it deeply, coughed, blinked. When he was recovered from this episode he said: "Well, I guess this is good-bye."

"Oh, Francis." Mrs. Weddings sighed. "You've left here a hundred times and never said good-bye. I can't believe it's good-bye now." She dropped her cigarette on the wooden porch and tapped it out with the toe of her favorite old slipper. "It's disappearing, running away, going off to find some more trouble to bring back to me."

"No," Francis told her. "This is not that."

Celeste, wearing an absurd gold-and-green-striped hat, approached them, extended her hand, and said: "Let me help you to the car, Francis." Mrs. Weddings smiled. She expected some sarcastic remark from her son, a wry, dismissive comment that edged toward cruel but stopped short; but Francis only took his sister's hand; and this gesture of restraint, this perfect intuition, Mrs. Weddings saw suddenly to be her son's real genius. She loved him so just then. She put three fingers to her chin and felt tears at her eyes.

She walked down the few steps, following her children. "Look at that moon, children," she said.

The moon was ice-white, its oceans and hills splendidly clear, and around the moon was a small circle of blue, and around that a larger ring of amber, all against a starless black sky. "Isn't it unbelievably beautiful, children?" asked the mother gently.

Francis entered the passenger side and laboriously seated himself, and Mrs. Weddings placed a blanket over his knees, tucked it tight. Everything was ready. The trip would only take an hour or so.

Celeste, though, was frozen, gazing upward at the astonishing, almost unreal moon. She was startled by this vision of the sky. She was mesmerized, for if she'd ever seen it look quite this way, that was long ago and she could not remember. Now it seemed a novelty. "Oh, my," said she, very softly, really to herself. "Oh, my."

A BETTER PLACE

RULES

Sunny, white dust through the enormous windows. Miss Dent, arranging things on her desk, was singing, softly, slowly, and out of tune: *I'm gonna love you, Like nobody's loved you, Come rain or come shine,* and she drew out the feeling of that last note as she'd heard those old singers do on the radio.

The workbooks and her lesson plans laid out before her, she took a step back, looked around the room, checking to see that everything was in order.

She heard the squealing sound of the bus as it pulled up to the school building, and that rubbery punch of the bus doors opening. Then she heard the voices: thin and high, a faraway sweet humming. Miss Dent loved children so much.

The children filed past her classroom window to the entrance of the school. Their voices grew louder and words became discernible. A girl shrieked: "I *hate* you!" then laughed. A boy was calling: "Danny, hey, Danny, hey, Danny, hey, come here, hey Danny." Miss Dent held her breath.

There was a mirror on the inside of her closet door. Miss Dent stood before it, patted down her pale red hair. She gazed at her eyes, leaned back a bit. Forever, since she was a little girl, Miss Dent had known how remarkable her eyes were, a light purple color, almost violet, almost lavender; people had always noticed the strange color of her eyes, and called her beautiful; forever, though, she had thought those gorgeous eyes just the slightest bit crossed, and at mirrors, at her reflection in store windows, she would stand away to check from a distance. And then her eyes would seem perfectly fine.

The bell rang. Miss Dent walked across her classroom. Miss Dent, with a quick breath, could conjure up competence, steel herself with a certain severe pose: the back of her hand on her side, the knuckles flat against the hip bone. She opened the door.

The children stood in two uneven lines, wearing light jackets, holding lunchboxes and bookbags. At the other end of the corridor, Mrs. Folsom's children waited at her door in a similar formation.

The faces of her class looked up at Miss Dent, blinking eyes, sniffling. Miss Dent spotted one girl wearing glasses that were mended with tape at the temples. Her attention was caught then by a boy who was taller than the other children, darker. His coat was open and there was a bandage on his chin.

"Come in, class," said Miss Dent, and she stood aside.

The children proceeded noisily, rushing to certain seats. The girl with the broken glasses passed and Miss Dent wanted to say "Good morning," but the girl kept her head down; she was wearing a green hat with a green ball on top. The boy with the bandage followed and looked up at Miss Dent. "How did you get hurt, young man?" Miss Dent asked. "Fell" was his answer, and he walked to the back of the room with an odd swagger, a phony meanness.

Down the hall, Mrs. Folsom's class was much more orderly as it marched inside her classroom, unified, silently disciplined somehow by Mrs. Folsom's severity: the woman had a squat, almost freakish frame, draped with a gray tailored suit, and she kept her arms folded across her sturdy bosom. Mrs. Folsom winked at Miss Dent, who smiled weakly.

Mrs. Folsom had been helpful in the teachers' lounge that morning: "Margie, here's one piece of advice to remember. Start mean. That's the trick with a class." Mrs. Folsom's hair was gray and black, elaborately styled with bangs and curls at the temples. She ran a plastic spoon around the inside of her yogurt cup for the last little bit, licked it off. Mrs. Folsom was intensely, deliberately calm. "The whole key is control," she went on. "They're clever, they're watching you. And if they think you're an easy mark—"

And Miss Dent was thinking, Well, they're only eight years old. . . .

"—your whole semester will be ruined. You can always soften up as time goes on. There'll be plenty of opportunity to make friends—with some of them, anyway. But start mean."

Miss Dent heard a giggle, then another. She was writing her name on the chalkboard; her back was to the class. She turned around. Several hands were covering mouths, heads were lowered, the children were peeking, there was a wash of tiny laughs across the room.

Miss Dent's slip was showing. She recalled then, in a vivid, jolting flash, her own third-grade teacher, Miss Crocker, recalled that bit of slip and giggling thirteen years ago.

Miss Dent tugged on her turquoise skirt.

"I am Miss Dent," said Miss Dent, looking over the heads of the seated children. "I would like to welcome all of you children to the third grade, and I am sure we're going to have a wonderful year together." Miss Dent placed the piece of chalk on its shelf under the board and took a few steps to her right, toward the flag.

"Now, in this classroom, it is very important that we have certain rules. So, we're going to spend a little time this morning going over our rules, the reasons for them, and any questions you might have."

Miss Dent did not look at any one face; her attention did not rest, but vaguely regarded the tops of the childrens' heads, the rows of desks, the globe in the corner.

"First of all," said she, "when you take your seats at the first bell, I want your coats and other garments hung in the little cloakroom over to the side"—Miss Dent pointed—"and your books and belongings placed inside your desks. I'm going to allow you to sit in the places you have chosen this morning. For now. But, if there are any problems, I'll have to assign seats." Miss Dent paused then, to let the fairness of this bargain be absorbed by the class. "Then, when you have taken your seats—quietly, please, and quickly—you will place your hands folded neatly on top of your desks."

The children were looking at her eyes, she knew, her slightly-crossed, striking violet eyes.

The desks were in three rows. Miss Dent began her walk up the right aisle, toward the back of the room, looking at each child as she passed. "Hands folded neatly on top of your desk please," Miss Dent instructed the first student, a stick-figure girl with uncombed blond hair. The girl did as she was told. Miss Dent smiled. "Very nice."

She walked on, and each child put arms on desktops, interlaced tiny fingers. Miss Dent came back along the left aisle.

Third desk down, that taller boy. "What is your name, young man?" she asked sternly.

"Andre." Andre had his hands in his pockets, his shoulders hunched. His eyes were light brown, his skin was a caramel color, his hair was a deep black that, in this light from the window, seemed to shine like steel.

"Andre, I've asked everyone to begin our day with hands folded neatly on desks. Do you think you can do that?"

"Guess so," answered the boy. He slowly locked his fingers, brought the hands against the desk, as though hitting it.

"Thank you, Andre," she said, and her smile was tight. Miss Dent felt at that moment exactly as teachers are supposed to feel; her bearing and manner controlled the children. She proceeded briskly to the front of the room, the hollow clicking of her heels the only sound, and it was a satisfying sound to her.

Miss Dent picked up her brand-new piece of chalk and faced the board. She wrote "Rules" and underlined the word. She wrote the number I and said: "Rule number one, class. No talking," and wrote those words in large script. She numbered, she wrote, and she spoke all the while, rather too loudly; she was remembering old Miss Crocker writing on the board, her back to the class, her butt wriggling and bouncing with each motion, a white end of her slip appearing now and again, the giggling.

No leaving your desk without permission. No going to the bathroom—you must go before class. No fighting. Always raise your hand when you wish to speak. Homework must be turned in on time. No copying from your neighbor's paper. No whispering.

Miss Dent turned back to face the children. She tugged at her turquoise skirt. "Now, class. Let's remember, we are not in the second grade anymore. This is the *third* grade. So, here are some rules we must follow in order to have an"—she could not think of a word—"an orderly classroom environment."

"What's 'enviramen'?" a voice asked.

Miss Dent did not look at any specific child; she did not know for certain who had spoken. "There will be *no* talking out of turn. If any of you have questions or comments, you will raise your hand and I will call on you."

A white limb waved from the center row.

"Yes, what is your name?"

"Mitchell. What's 'enviramen'?"

Miss Dent was struck with panic, as if a match had burned her fingers, but she did not want to show pain. What *is* environment? Very slowly: "Well, Mitchell, environment means . . . this room."

She took a deep breath and abruptly turned her attention away from Mitchell's puzzled expression.

"So, we'll begin now with a little assignment. I want all of you to take out your notebooks and a pencil. Head your papers—I want your name and today's date, which I have written on the board. And I want you each to copy down the rules I have listed on the board, and then write down two more rules of your own. Make up rules that you think are important for the class."

A hand went up in the far left corner. Miss Dent lifted her chin. "Yes?"

"Do the rules we make up have to be different ones from the ones up there?" The inquirer was a petite, beautiful black girl, dressed in a pink dress, with pink ribbons at the ends of her braids. She was smiling wide.

"What is your name, dear?"

"Loretta."

"Loretta, were you listening to my instructions?" The girl gave two sharp nods of her head. "I don't think you were, Loretta. What I told the class was that you must all *copy* down the rules I have put on the board. And then I want you to *think* of two more rules, all your *own*, that would be good to have in this class."

Loretta still smiled; it was clear she didn't fully understand. Miss Dent thought, How can she not understand this? And she turned away, looked above all the heads, toward the enormous windows at the back of the room. "Any other questions? Fine. Now in a few moments, we will have a class discussion about the importance of rules."

She heard the sound of pencils on paper. She saw the girl with the taped glasses, seated at the front in the first row, looking at the ceiling, biting the eraser.

"Class," said Miss Dent, "I am stepping out of the room for one minute and I want you all to remain seated and working on your papers." She quietly opened the door and stepped into the corridor.

Just next to Miss Dent's classroom was a storage room where textbooks were kept. Miss Dent stepped inside. She locked the door behind her. She slid the window open a crack. She took a cigarette and lighter from her skirt pocket, lit it, inhaled deeply several times, fast, blew smoke out the window, fanned the air with her other hand.

Mrs. Folsom had told her: "Some of them love to do everything perfectly, they look up at you, they want approval, stroking, stroking for being good. Those are easier to deal with, naturally. You adore them, you're proud of them. But there's something strange and sad about them, too. I almost like the troublemakers more, myself."

HOME

It took Miss Dent exactly thirty minutes to drive from the Clara Barton Elementary School to the Oasis Motel, where she was temporarily staying in room number 21. Miss Dent's age was also twenty-one.

The journey was straight through flat desert; on either side stretched light brown sand, bits of brush, rock: an endless, dusty, colorless drive. She left the school at three o'clock, so the sun was still high. She wore dark glasses.

Inside room 21, Miss Dent pulled open the heavy orange drapes. "Aren't I lucky to be on the second floor?" she said. From her window she could see a heart-shaped swimming pool, its water bright green and still. There were orange lounge chairs placed round the pool. All the motel-room doors were orange, and the sign at the entrance was an elaborate orange neon palm tree and the word OASIS blinking orange.

She undid the snaps at the side of her skirt to loosen it and kicked her low-heeled shoes into a corner. She lit a cigarette and stood at her window until she spotted a tabby cat trotting across the courtyard below, past the pool, toward the motel office. "I hate cats," she said, and turned away. She stretched out on her back, diagonally across the double bed with the orange-and-yellow spread. She closed her eyes.

"I'm not happy here," Miss Dent whispered. "Can I be happy in this place?"

The country all around her was dust and orange and sand, low brick buildings, shining under a relentless sun; the air was windless.

She was remembering herself on a cool night last year, wearing a new dress and coat, riding the subway to meet her friends in the city. And she'd had a date with Mark that night, to go dancing.

She was a fun girl, she was a quick and busy girl; she laughed loud and liked to drink, not too much, but enough to be laughing and fun and free.

She was a redhead. She liked to have a good time. She liked flirting, teasing.

In the back of a taxi, Mark got sweaty, she felt him get hard against her leg; she laughed as she said good night.

Miss Dent missed her friends. She missed the city. She missed elevators and vendors. The faces of all those friends were before her now. Their faces described who she was. This orange, dry landscape, these tedious people—she did not belong here.

Miss Dent opened her eyes. Finally, the sun was losing its brilliance, hazy in the cloudless pale blue sky.

She swung her legs around and put her feet on the floor. She picked up the orange telephone receiver. "Yes, operator, this is Miss Dent in twenty-one. I'd like to make a long-distance call. New York City." She said the number and lit a cigarette. She smiled, she was feeling better; for the moment was near, the moment when she would hear the voice of her best friend, Gloria, her very best friend since they were babies. Four-thirty here, so it was six-thirty Gloria's time. So Gloria was probably getting dressed to go out for dinner.

"Gloria? Gloria? Hey, it's me, Margie. Well, I'm *fine.* God, how are *you?* How's everything going? Really? You're kidding. Well, I knew you'd get it, you've worked there a year already. Me, well, God, I don't know. It's very beautiful down here. I mean, it's all desert and little cactuses, just gorgeous. Today was my first day at the school. I don't know, they kind of leave you on your own, you know, I feel like I'm just kind of thrown in with these fourteen children and I have to feel my way through it. I've only even met the principal once, this guy Mr. Escoffier. Escoffier, like the sauce. And the building is this boring modern kind of building, brick, plain. It doesn't smell like schools are supposed to smell, you know? But it'll be fine. I have to just feel my way, get to know people, get to know the kids. The kids are just adorable, really sweet kids. I teach them reading and drawing and stuff and then they go off to this other teacher who does math. So I think it's going to be just this fabulous adventure, really; it's only adjusting that's hard. Feeling my way. Well, no, that apartment didn't come through, so I'm staying at this motel outside of town. It's called the Oasis Motel and everything's bright orange, it's really a scream, it's the silliest place. But I'm comfortable here for now. There's this one teacher, Mrs. Folsom, she's been teaching there for a hundred years or something, and she looks exactly like Miss Crocker. Remember Miss Crocker from third grade?" Miss Dent was laughing, she was seeing how really queer her new situation was, the motel, the dust and desert; she was so happy to be holding Gloria in her hand this way. "Then there's this other one, her name's Audrey St. Thomas, oh, God, and she's about my age but she's getting divorced, she always has a crisis going on, she's always complaining about everything. She wears these huge glasses and she's allergic to everything. She told me she was allergic to chalk, even. You'd die if you— What? Oh, oh, sure."

Gloria's doorbell had rung and she went to answer it. Miss Dent puffed her cigarette, waiting. "Hello? Oh, it's Greg. Well, tell him hello from me, okay? Yes, I just felt like calling. No, I understand. I can't talk too much longer either, really, because I have to prepare lessons for tomorrow. So, listen, have a great time tonight. Say hello from me to everyone. Okay, Gloria. Talk to you soon."

Miss Dent turned on the television news. A blond weather girl, standing before a map, smiled and said it would be fair, no rain. Miss Dent turned the T.V. off.

Miss Dent drew the drapes closed. She lay across her bed again. "I always do that," Miss Dent whispered. "I always say how everything's fine, or it's all going to be fine." She blinked at the ceiling, felt tears at the corners of her remarkable eyes, a tiny pounding pulse at her temples.

She did not wake until after sunset. The sky was deep, dark blue, full of stars. She looked through her drapes and saw people down at the pool, heard a woman's high-pitched laugh.

Then it was money on Miss Dent's mind. Her car had had trouble on the trip West, and that had cost so much. She had put a deposit on an apartment in town, secured through some friend of Gloria's, but it didn't work out, the story was so convoluted and embarrassing and Miss Dent still had not got back her deposit. On motel stationery, she made a list of her finances: her room was twenty-nine dollars a night, eating at the restaurant was another six or seven, then gas, cigarettes.

She had less than a hundred dollars left. How could she find an apartment? And she wouldn't get paid until the end of the month. "Seems like I spend a hundred dollars just in that soda machine every day," Miss Dent said, and smiled.

Miss Dent put on her gold robe—a gift from Mark—and slippers. She went out into the cool night, walked the length of the balcony toward the soda and candy and ice machines, carrying her orange plastic ice bucket in her arms.

From below she heard a man's deep voice: "She'll fuck anything that moves." Two or three women laughed, and one said: *"Sam!"*

"No, seriously," said the man, "dead seriously, this chick will fuck anyone, anywhere, anytime, and then beg for more."

Miss Dent was quick about getting her ice and cans of soda, stole as quietly as she could back into her room.

She turned on the television. "They've got to have some old movies or something. Or an old *Perry Mason* or something." What appeared on screen was a smiling dark-haired man in a suit, standing before a satellite picture of earth, reassuring that tomorrow would be fair, there would be no rain.

WORK

"Why do we read books?" The class was seated in a circle on the floor, and a few arms shot up, hands waved. "Class, I've told you, you don't need to wave your hands like that. I'm right here, I can see all of you. Now, then. Eugene?"

"That they always tell stories?"

"All right, yes, we read books sometimes because they tell us stories. Anyone else? Margaret?"

The girl with the taped glasses barely lifted her head. Her hair was thin, a dull brown, parted in the center. "To learn about other countries because sometimes the books tell about other countries."

Mitchell said: "I like kings and queens."

"You've spoken out of turn again, Mitchell," said Miss Dent sternly, and the little boy immediately put both hands over his mouth.

"Sorry," he said.

"It's fine to be sorry, it's nice that you're sorry, Mitchell. But, you must learn to think before you talk." Miss Dent gazed for a significant second of reprimand. She thought, Can't they understand *anything*, can't they get one goddamn thing through their heads?

She continued: "We were talking about why we read books. Does anyone else have any ideas? Andre, what about you?"

"Cause they make us."

The other children laughed.

Miss Dent had had enough from Andre. Miss Dent had had enough; just as Miss Crocker all those years before had had enough. She remembered the sight of Miss Crocker: that terrifying adult frustration, the singular purpose in her arched brow, how tall she had seemed, and the stiff walk across the classroom to her desk. Miss Dent became Miss Crocker now.

She told the class to return to their seats and bring out their grammar notebooks, and then she said: "Andre, I will see you at my desk, please." There was a murmur among the students.

Miss Dent sat in the wooden chair at her desk, and Andre walked slowly, his hands in his pockets, to stand beside her.

Their eyes were level. "Andre, we are having some serious problems, aren't we?"

"I guess so."

"You guess so? Well, it has been over almost two months now into our semester. The Christmas break will be here before we know it. What have you been doing in class all this time, Andre?"

"I've been doing things."

Miss Dent simply did not like Andre. She'd no affection for him whatever. He was bigger than the others; he seemed dirty, as though he didn't bathe. She had heard him making fun of her. And all children did that, all children made fun, even she had laughed at Miss Crocker all those years ago; but the meanness in Andre was deep. When it came to this Andre she felt a peculiar powerlessness: none of the accepted teacher threats, no severity, no sort of challenge or appeal could get through to Andre. She had several times said she would have to call his parents, and Andre's expression, that bored half-smile, was unchanged.

"Well," said she, flipping through a folder of papers on her desk, "I look at what you've been doing in class so far, Andre. You don't have a single star next to your name. You see here"—she pushed a paper toward him—"you see how Mitchell has three stars, Eugene and Paul have stars, Loretta has all those stars next to her name, and Margaret? No stars for you, Andre." Andre shrugged.

She went on: "You also have seven tardy marks. You have been sent to Mr. Escoffier three times. And I had to give you an X for the spelling bee because you would not practice with the rest of the class. Do you have anything to say about all of this, Andre?"

Miss Dent had brought Mitchell to her desk a couple of weeks before to discipline him for always talking out of turn, and Mitchell had stood staring at the floor, twisting his fingers, and very suddenly started to cry. Miss Dent was completely surprised; she'd handed the boy a tissue. She'd considered hugging him, but could not.

This Andre, though, nothing could make him cry. "At the rate you're going, Andre, I don't think you're going to make it into the fourth grade." This prospect she knew to be a chilling one for her students; Mrs. Folsom had recommended such a threat in extreme cases. Andre, though, only blinked.

Miss Dent was angrier now, and dying for a cigarette. "Well, young man, I'm going to write a little note to your mother and I want you to give it to her when you go home tonight." With her red pen, she scribbled out a request for an appointment, said the matter was very urgent, signed her name, tore the paper from the pad, and folded it. She held it out to Andre. "Is that understood?"

Andre took the paper, put it in the back pocket of his loose, soiled jeans, and returned to his seat.

Miss Dent stood, put her fingertips on her desk, leaned forward, and said, too loudly: "Children, I have to step out of the room for a moment. You should all be looking over the vocabulary words from yesterday, because some of you will be asked to do spelling on the board. So I want no talking while I'm gone."

In the book room, she lit her cigarette and blew smoke out the window. "Oh, I can't stand that little Andre," she whispered. "Snotty little bastard. I would love to see him break down in tears in front of the whole class." She lit another cigarette with the butt end of her first one, because then she was back to thinking about money. In the time she'd been in this godforsaken place, she had simply not been able to save, not been able to get ahead. She would cash her check and pay her bills and barely have enough for cigarettes and gas until her next check. Well, Gloria could lend me money, she thought, if it comes down to that. It would take a few days in the mail. This motel room is eating up my whole salary, and then they take so much taxes out.

Miss Dent suddenly was pouting furiously, holding back tears, as she realized she'd not even a few dollars in her purse for lunch in the cafeteria today.

By the end of the morning she had had to send Andre to Mr. Escoffier's office. Now, in the teachers' lounge with Mrs. St. Thomas, Miss Dent was chain-smoking and sipping weak coffee. The room was sparsely furnished with mismatched, straight-back chairs around a gray table, and a sink and refrigerator were against one wall.

"They don't care," Mrs. St. Thomas was saying, as she unwrapped her tuna-fish sandwich. "These kids just don't care."

Miss Dent did not want to sound too irritated. "I gave Andre a note for his mother. I told his mother I want to meet with her."

"Now, that's assuming he'll even give the note to his mother. I'm telling you, these kids just don't care." Mrs. St. Thomas had a bit of the white creamy tuna at the corner of her mouth, but did not notice. "When I was teaching the fourth-grade music classes, I was sending four or five of them to the principal's office every day. Notes home, phone calls. Ended up having a whole set of recorders stolen. Brand new. These kids are not the same as when we were children." She leaned back in her chair and called out into the hallway: "Hey, you, where are you supposed to be?"

A brown-skinned boy of ten or so appeared in the doorway of the teachers' lounge. "Mr. Poole said I could go to the bathroom."

"I don't care who said what. Did he give you a hall pass?" barked Mrs. St. Thomas.

The boy stuttered: "But Mr. Poole said—"

"You march back and get a hall pass." She turned back to Miss Dent. "You see? Little liar. And that Elliot Poole is no better than some of these kids. First of all, he's not exactly what you'd call a very manly man, if you know what I mean. He's not married, if you know what I mean. And here he is with the young boys. Teaching science, no less."

Mrs. St. Thomas rose then, neatly tucked half of her sandwich in a paper bag, and placed it on the bottom shelf of the refrigerator. She left the lounge, saying: "See you at the buses."

Miss Dent was alone. Some classes were at lunch, some on the playground. "I'm lonely," said she. "That's what it is. I miss my friends. This is no kind of life." She thought, but did not say aloud, that she was afraid of the children. Because she did not understand them. Skinny boys kept their arms folded across their chests. Wiry, tough, sloppy boys. Girls giggled, made up rhymes. Some child was always ready to indict another—"I saw her chewing gum, Miss Dent"; "Miss Dent, he said a bad word." That little Margaret always wanted to hold her hand on the playground; Loretta or Mitchell always had to use the bathroom. Shy ones, needy ones, pouting and lies, uncomprehending blinks, and then crying; at least one of them cried every day. And whispers, infuriating whispers from every corner. *No whispering*, she had told them.

Miss Dent was discovering that she did not possess what the other teachers seemed to, a sense of herself in relation to the children, a knowledge of her power and place. Some mornings, facing the sunny windows, the rows of heads, Miss Dent feared every motion and breath, any assertion. She felt like a ghost.

She felt like a ghost. Without thinking much, she walked to the refrigerator, opened it, stuck her arm in, felt around for the bag with Mrs. St. Thomas' half sandwich, and removed it. She tore a piece of paper towel from a roll on the counter, hurriedly wrapped the sandwich, and dropped it in her purse. The bell rang. Miss Dent headed back to her classroom.

At three o'clock, Miss Dent was standing in the parking lot with the other teachers, supervising the lines of children. Some went home by bus, some waited separately for their parents to pick them up. Mr. Poole had a flat ass and glasses; he was going bald. Today, Mrs. Folsom was wearing a brown skirt and jacket with a cactus pin at the breast.

Mrs. St. Thomas was beside Miss Dent. She blew a piercing, horrifying whistle and shouted across the lot: "Danny Stranger and Gary Harding if you two don't stand still I'm going to separate you! Penny, you too, just stand quietly in line, please. No, you don't need to ask Allison anything, you just need to stay in line." To Miss Dent, then:

"That Penny and Allison drive me crazy. Did I tell you my ceiling caved in? Came home yesterday afternoon, was all in a rush because I had a meeting with Arthur's lawyer and my lawyer, and I was all in a rush and I walked in my kitchen door and the ceiling has this huge hole and plaster was all over everything. *Everything.* That's the last thing I need, right?" She was distracted suddenly by some commotion among the children. She blew her whistle. "Uh, Leonard, this is not playtime, this is not recess. Where are you supposed to be? Is that what you're supposed to be doing? Is that the line you're supposed to be in? Well, get where you're supposed to be."

When the buses had gone, Miss Dent walked briskly down the center of the corridor, imitating Miss Crocker's feared stride. On either wall were bulletin boards with children's artwork pinned to them, letters cut out of different-colored construction paper spelling AUTUMN, and crayon drawings of leaves. She listened to the echoing of her heels as she walked. She thought miserably, They don't even *have* leaves here.

As she approached the front office she saw the school plaque: a silhouette of Clara Barton, the name of the school, the names of past principals engraved.

"Night, Miss Dent," said Vilma, and she coughed. Vilma had been the school secretary at Clara Barton Elementary for thirteen years. She was the only member of faculty or staff permitted to smoke cigarettes outside of the teachers' lounge. She wore slacks and sweaters and read mystery novels at her desk.

"Yes, goodnight, Vilma," Miss Dent responded. She turned to look in her mailbox and saw little Margaret, sitting on a bench, her book bag beside her. "Well, hello, Margaret," said Miss Dent, pulling envelopes from the box with her name on it. She took her time card from its slot in the IN rack, punched it through the clock, placed it in the OUT rack. "And what are we doing in the office, Margaret?"

Margaret kept her head lowered, but raised her eyes. She pulled a strand of hair that had gotten caught between her lips. "I don't know."

Miss Dent sat next to Margaret, kept her papers and letters on her lap. "I see you got your glasses fixed. They look very pretty."

"Her mother's late," came from Vilma behind the counter, and a pancake of cigarette smoke rose and settled.

"Your mother usually picks you up, is that it?"

"Yes, she picks me up, but she forgot to today so I have to wait."

Margaret's scarf was wrapped tightly round her neck; she seemed too restricted by her dull plaid coat and the green hat with the green ball on top.

Miss Dent said: "Well, I'm sure Mother will be along any minute now." Miss Dent rose. She looked down at the girl.

Vilma, a cigarette hanging from the corner of her lips, was rolling paper through a typewriter. "So don't you worry, Margaret," said Miss Dent. The little girl did not reply, did not look up. She swung her bare legs back and forth.

Miss Dent hurried back down the wide corridor, toward the glass doors at its end, which led to the parking lot. Sweet little girl, Miss Dent was thinking, shy and sweet, troubled, doesn't seem to have many friends, I never see her playing. Miss Dent's car pulled away in a shower of pebbles and dust, and she headed toward home.

DREAMS

Dear Mark,

It was so sweet of you to send me a postcard. Hawaii looks delicious! And it's funny you say you can picture me with a bun in my hair and a ruler in my hand, because it's almost just like that! No, really—teaching is going so well, better than I could have dreamed. I just have to feel my way for a while. I'm still looking for a better place to live.

Someone dove into the pool. A woman was laughing.

Miss Dent was sadly missing her friends, longing to be with them, taking up a table all night at a diner, laughing. She'd phoned Gloria a few times, but Gloria had not returned the call.

So, I heard about Gloria and Greg getting married. I'm really going to try to get back for the wedding. It's in June, right? I have not made plans for the summer yet. Travel, maybe.

Some kind of animal moans in the desert in the evening, a coyote or something, and you can't tell how close it is.

Anyway, all goes well here. Working with children is such an extraordinary experience, so rich. . . . I am learning all the time, discovering. And the countryside is so marvelous, breathtaking. I know, I know, everyone thought I was so crazy to come out here. But, you know me—always ready for some new thing. I'm starting to make some friends among the other teachers, and even

Miss Dent abruptly stopped writing her letter with the panicked realization that she had *no* money, not one dollar. She yanked her purse across the bed and looked through it.

"Goddamn it," she said, "goddamn it, goddamn it. I'm going to starve in this fucking wasteland." She slid the pen and her letter into the drawer of the bedside table, on top of the motel's courtesy Bible. She leaned back, put her hands to her forehead.

Later that night, Miss Dent, seated at the desk, took a break from grading her papers and considered what she might say to Andre's mother. She whispered: "I must tell you that Andre's behavior has been absolutely unacceptable. He's a distraction to the class. He's moody, he acts up." Miss Dent gazed at her face in the mirror. She looked tired, her red hair was mussed. She had freak eyes, she thought.

She lit a cigarette. "Andre is not living up to his potential. He's a bright boy, but he doesn't push himself. He comes unprepared to class, he talks back and bothers the other children. Now, don't cry, dear. We'll just have to keep Andre in the third grade. He's not ready to move on. He's a fucking little monster"—Miss Dent saw her half-lit dull reflection start to laugh—"he's a moron little asshole squirt and we're going to have to punish him, extreme, severe punishment, and then when he cries and begs me for forgiveness—in the mirror, she saw her shoulders rolling forward and back in a rhythm with her laughter— "when he's down on his knees naked and covered with bloody welts, we'll pass your boy into the fourth grade."

That night, Miss Dent slept fully clothed. She dreamed of the desert, cool but windless, and she was making her way across the coarse sand in bare feet; and then she was trying to plant flowers in the sand. Someone—Mrs. Folsom, maybe, but she was too tall to be Mrs.

Folsom—told her that kind of flower wouldn't grow in the desert, and Miss Dent cried.

Another dream was about Loretta, her favorite, the sweetest child, the neatest, that striking little girl with rich chocolate-colored skin and pink bows; it was a pleasant, joyful dream, there was laughter, there was a thick green meadow such as did not really exist for miles and miles. But, when she woke, a bit late, Miss Dent was uneasy and disoriented. Through dreaming of the child, she felt she knew her too well, had seen her too close. When she thought of being near Loretta in the classroom, she was embarrassed. She did not want these children in her dreams, she did not.

She lit a cigarette and turned on the television news. Garbo's death. Greta Garbo, dead at eighty-something, in New York City. The announcer read a list of her fabulous films and said she had been extremely reclusive for over fifty years. Her most striking and famous photographs were shown, and old Hollywood friends and colleagues were interviewed. All about her talent and beauty. The greatest screen actress. And some old director with a German accent said: "Oh, we'll miss her so very much. It is a great loss. But I know she's gone to a better place."

They always say that, Miss Dent reflected, when people die. That they've gone to a better place. They always say that and it always feels so hopeless and awful. What is the point of struggling through this life if there will be such a better one when we've died?

Thank God, today was payday. Miss Dent had not even enough money for gas. When would she ever get ahead? When would she have enough to look for an apartment or a room for rent? When would she ever get out of this ridiculous motel? Miss Dent changed hurriedly, combed her hair. She sped and was at the school well before the first bell.

INNOCENCE

Just after lunch period, Miss Dent and her class were working on syllables. "Florence, can you tell us how many syllables are in the word 'walking'?"

"Three?"

Miss Dent frowned, squinted. "Does anybody have the *correct* answer to my question? Yes, Paul."

Paul said the word had one syllable, then beamed with assurance. He was missing a tooth.

"No, no, Miss Dent, no," cried out Mitchell, raising his hand and waving.

"Mitchell, what have I told you about calling out? Do you know the answer?"

"It's got two sibabels."

Miss Dent ordered the children to the art table to scribble with crayons. They had ten minutes, and then all classes were to assemble in the auditorium for a nature film.

Miss Dent went for a smoke in the book room. "I mean, do they ever learn even the simplest things? I mean, how in the world do they ever manage?" She'd become careless with her cigarettes over the months, barely directing the smoke out the window, and she was unaware, too, of how loudly she was speaking. "Don't their parents ever read to them, or talk to them, or anything? It's like they're a bunch of hopeless idiots."

The door to the book room was suddenly opened. "Oh. Oh, I . . ." It was Mr. Poole. Miss Dent's mouth was open, her arms folded over her chest, one hand extended with the cigarette between two fingers. Mr. Poole backed away slightly, then moved into the room. "I'm sorry to interrupt. I needed . . . I'm looking for an extra science text." He scanned the shelves quickly. Miss Dent did not move.

Mr. Poole took a volume from a box on the floor. "Ah, good. I'm one short. Well, I guess, I guess, well . . ."

He turned to leave, was closing the door behind him, and Miss Dent said: "Elliot?"

"Yes, Margie?" He peeked in at her. He had thick glasses and a long, skinny neck.

"Elliot, you won't tell on me, will you?"

Mr. Poole shook his head and was gone.

Rubbing her forehead, Miss Dent analyzed: They're these innocent little *creatures.* They're unformed, they're pure. They're just learning everything, all about the world, nature. They have yet to deal with money and sex and careers. It's all immediate to them. They have absolutely no decisions to make.

She ground the cigarette onto the floor with her shoe. I mean, really, that is the spookiest thing, they have no decisions to make, no choices. They just go along. When they want something, they either get it or they cry or whatever. They're like animals. They're all response, all moods and feelings, they have not learned to interpret their impressions. There's no filter between them and the world. They're happy or they're sad.

"They're just happy, or they're sad, or they're angry," Miss Dent said, astonished.

The class was seated and strangely silent when Miss Dent returned. "Well?" she asked, of no particular child. "Well? Why aren't you all at the art table?"

There was silence.

"What is going on here? Paul? Melissa?"

Melissa said something softly, her hands covering her mouth.

"People can't understand you when you mumble behind your mouth, Melissa." The students were uncommonly somber, furtively exchanging glances with each other.

Miss Dent took a harsh step toward Mitchell's desk. "Mitchell, what has happened?"

Mitchell leaned his head all the way back to look up at his teacher. "Andre hit Margaret."

Several of the children were talking then—"I saw it, Miss Dent," and "Miss Dent, Margaret was crying, her glasses got knocked off"— and Miss Dent turned to the back of the room, saw through the streams of sun and dust Andre's black hair, his slouching posture as he leaned on the two back legs of his chair. She moved to him, bent over him, stared fiercely. "Do you sit on chairs at home like that?" she found herself asking.

Andre rocked forward so his chair was upright.

"And is it true you hit Margaret?"

"Accident," said Andre.

"What kind of accident?" she asked, leaning in closer so her face was directly in front of his.

"It was by mistake," said Andre.

"I am tired of your mistakes, young man." She slapped his desk with her hand. Behind Miss Dent there was a gasping sound, the students startled, and it was a queer pleasure to her.

"I am goddamn sick and tired of you, do you hear me?" She was yelling now.

"She said 'G-D'." someone whispered.

"You don't want to behave decently in here and get along with the others? You can just get the fuck out of my classroom," Miss Dent shrieked, and then a couple of children were crying, but frozen and fearful. The students were tragically lost at this moment, without alliance.

Miss Dent pushed two hands against Andre's chest and turned sharply away from him. She walked to her desk. She was not calmed, she was still enraged. She moved some books from one side of her desk to the other.

She looked out the huge window at the lonely, dry landscape, cracked earth dotted with brown and pale green. After a moment, she turned to face her class.

She looked at each desk, confused. "Where is Margaret now?"

No one would answer. She tried to speak slowly, to seem soft. "Does anybody know where Margaret went? Did she go to the nurse?"

Miss Dent walked the length of the room and out the door. She stood in the corridor, listening. She lit a cigarette. She heard the music class practicing recorders.

She'd gone to the office, Miss Dent reckoned, or to the nurse or somewhere. Miss Dent, now puffing her cigarette unashamedly, moved quickly to the staircase at the end of the corridor. All the school's railings were made specially low, for children; she grasped the railing with both hands, pulled herself upward, two steps at a time, as though she were climbing a hillside; her hair fell across her eyes. "My name is Margaret, too," Miss Dent was saying, a breathless incantation propel-

ling her upward. She listened for voices, for footsteps. At the second
floor she whispered loudly: "Margaret?"

Mr. Poole immediately opened his door and popped his head out.
"Something wrong?"

Miss Dent did not answer, nor look at the man. She continued up
the stairs, crossed the landing.

And there was Margaret sitting on the top step, before the door to
the roof. Her head was on her knees, cradled in her thin, white arms.
Her feet, in black patent-leather Mary Janes, were turned inward, and
her glasses, in two pieces, rested between them.

"Oh, Margaret," said Miss Dent. "Oh, dear, I was very worried
about you." She sat on the step just below the child. Margaret did not
lift her head.

"I know all about what happened. Andre hit you, I know all about
it. You mustn't cry, now. It's all over. Will you look at me, Margaret?"
The child would not. "You know, my name is Margaret, too. Margaret
Dent, that's my name. And people always call me Margie. Maybe you
want to be called Margie."

Miss Dent held the child's elbows gently, then, lifted her slowly. "I
tell you what. We're going out here on the roof for a nice breath of
air. Just you and me, Margie. Have a little talk, and try and see if you
don't feel better."

Miss Dent pushed open the door, stepped out onto the gravel-and-
tar roof. "Come out with me, Margie."

Margaret held the broken glasses in both of her hands as though they
were pieces of something beautiful and rare that had to be saved; she
followed her teacher out onto the roof, stumbling on the step. Miss
Dent laughed a sweet, generous laugh. "Oh, you can't see too well
without your glasses," she said, and led the girl by the hand.

"Oh, isn't it beautiful up here? Like we're way above the rest of the
world, isn't it?"

Margaret nodded and sniffled, kept her eyes lowered.

Miss Dent told Margaret to take a nice deep breath. She told her
that Andre would be punished, that he was a bad boy, that Margaret
did not have to worry about him anymore. "That's a promise," said
Miss Dent.

Suddenly, Margaret's tiny shoulders were shaking, she sobbed and
swallowed, tears streamed down her cheeks.

Miss Dent knelt and held Margaret by the shoulders. "What, dear? Don't you believe me that everything will be all right?"

"It's that . . . it's that . . . I'm afraid . . . because," the child stammered. Even in this most tender and compassionate of moments, Miss Dent badly craved a cigarette and felt impatient with the girl's inarticulation, and said a bit harshly: *"What,* Margaret? What's the matter?"

"My glasses. They got broke and my mother'll be so mad."

Miss Dent hugged the child stiffly. "Oh, little Margie, don't you worry. I'll explain everything to your mother."

For the first time, Margaret looked at Miss Dent, directly into those fascinating, queer purple eyes. "You will?"

"Of course. Now let's get back downstairs. Everyone will be wondering what happened to us, won't they?"

Margaret nodded. They proceeded toward the roof door. Margaret took a step down. As Miss Dent turned to secure the door, she said: "And we want to see the nature film, don't we?"

It sounded like a box being dropped from a great height, or like a flat tire, or books falling from a shelf, or a carton of eggs smashing. Once, in high school, Gloria and Margie and some of the kids had dropped a carton of eggs from a window and nearly hit an old man, and they'd laughed.

It was Margaret, at the bottom of the flight of cement steps. Her legs were twisted, her arms folded above her head, that dull brown hair fanned out behind her. When Miss Dent reached the child, she saw blood coming from the corner of the mouth. The eyes were closed. Miss Dent could not touch her.

"Margie? Margie?"

RESPONSIBILITY

Miss Dent hurried into the side entrance of the auditorium. Mrs. Folsom was instantly beside her, speaking in a severe, husky tone which frightened Miss Dent. "I brought your children down for you, where were you? Mr. Escoffier was getting impatient, we have this film to show."

Mrs. St. Thomas appeared then. "Projector broke anyway. I swear, the equipment in this school is so outdated. So where were you?"

"I was looking for Margaret," Miss Dent explained. "You know little Margaret? Well, a boy in my class, Andre—"

From Mrs. St. Thomas: "Oh, that Andre's a real stinker."

"Well," Miss Dent went on, whispering, watching Mr. Escoffier, who was threading the film projector at the back of the auditorium, "apparently he hit the little girl. And she left the room crying. I've been looking all over for her. I'm very worried."

"You mean you can't find one of your children?" asked Mrs. St. Thomas seriously, softly.

Miss Dent nodded.

Mrs. Folsom abruptly turned and walked to Mr. Escoffier. That was exactly the walk Miss Crocker had had. Mrs. Folsom whispered in the principal's ear. Mr. Escoffier joined the teachers at the doorway and instructed Mrs. St. Thomas to lead the assembled children in some rhyming games or songs. He hurried out of the auditorium.

Mrs. Folsom looked at Miss Dent. "I'd say you had better follow him, Miss Dent," said she.

Miss Dent said: "Of course," and as she was leaving the large room, she looked behind, saw the backs of the heads of her class, saw Andre's shiny black hair and his arms resting on the seat beside him.

"What exactly occurred?" Mr. Escoffier asked Miss Dent as they reached the office. Vilma lit a cigarette and leaned forward on her elbows.

Miss Dent recounted the story she'd told the other teachers.

Vilma telephoned the nurse's office. "Not there," she informed Miss Dent and Mr. Escoffier. "Want me to call her mother?"

"Not just yet, not just yet," said the principal, flustered. "Miss Dent, I must say you leaving your classroom for such an extended period is not very responsible."

"Oh, I know, I know that. I assumed Margaret would be in the bathroom, or just down the hall, and when I couldn't find her anywhere . . ."

Mr. Escoffier passed into his private office and picked up the phone. He spoke with Mr. Murphy, the custodian. Then he turned on the switch for the public-address system: "Will Margaret"—he covered the microphone and asked Vilma the child's last name—"will Margaret Millhouse please come to the school office at once."

They waited. He repeated the announcement. They waited and heard the children singing about spiders and frogs. Miss Dent was desperate for one of Vilma's cigarettes.

At twenty minutes to three, Vilma told Mr. Escoffier: "Look, you got to call the kid's mother," and the principal, dejected, repressing his panic, agreed.

The children were lined up for their buses, and the teachers had punched out. Mrs. St. Thomas and Miss Dent stood together in front of the school.

"I remember a kid got stuck in the garbage chute here a few years ago. Not that that's where this little Mary is. They closed up those chutes."

"It's Margaret, her name is Margaret."

Mrs. St. Thomas put a hand on Miss Dent's arm. "Hey, listen. Listen, they'll find her. I know you must really be out of your mind with worry."

Miss Dent nodded.

PRAYER

For long, sad moments, there was no sound at all. Then Miss Dent could hear the low tones and laughing, splashing, the frivolous, irrelevant activity at the pool beneath her window.

Miss Dent's drapes were drawn. Miss Dent wore her robe and was seated in the orange chair; she had pulled it over so she could rest her feet on the edge of the bed. She had finished three cans of soda. She had been smoking cigarettes for hours, and a comforting gray cloud stayed still around her head.

"Dear God," said Miss Dent. She rested her head against the chair's cushioned back, let her eyes close. Her beautiful lilac-colored eyes were burning, sore from smoke and dust and dimness.

"Can anyone hear me?" Miss Dent asked. "Is there anyone out there to hear this small voice, this tired voice? It seems like I'm on another planet and it's too bright and hot here. I'm an alien." Miss Dent was whispering: "No one knows." She smiled, lit another cigarette and dropped the burning match into the glass ashtray, watched the flame die and its thin curl of smoke rise, disappear.

When Miss Dent was a little girl she was driven to prayer. She would lock the door to her room, kneel on the floor beside her bed, and hold her palms together. She would be in trouble, or worried, or sad and all she could think to do, finally, was to pray.

And now, her voice hoarse, her throat sore: "God, I know what I have done. I know I've done such a horrible, horrible thing. And I'll be punished, I know that. My punishment will be that this pain I'm feeling now will never go away."

Miss Dent turned her head, raised her shoulder to her chin, pulled in her elbows. "I'll die here, this way. I'll be this way from now on, and die like this, here. Here."

Laughter from the pool, a playful female scream, a splash, a splash.

"It was an accident, God. I didn't push her. She couldn't see too well, she fell. I don't think it was really my fault, and if I did do something, if somehow I caused it, it wasn't on purpose. I didn't mean to. So I want to be forgiven." She placed a hand on her cheek. "Protect me, God. Don't let me get caught, don't let them find out I was with the child. I know everything now. I know I'm not competent. I'm not smart or better than anyone. I have not felt any love in my life. I did not love that little girl. I don't love children, I know that. I've seen who I am, God. I'm still a child myself. Please, don't let anyone find out . . . about me."

Miss Dent had stood perfectly sober and concerned when Margaret's mother arrived at the school. Margaret's mother was some kind of businesswoman; she wore a cream-colored tailored suit and high heels, carried an attaché case. She was not at all hysterical, not even crying; she appeared mostly to be angry. Mr. Escoffier put his arm around her shoulder. Vilma gave her coffee. Mrs. St. Thomas was whispering to Mr. Poole.

But Miss Dent did not move or speak. She watched, breathing quick, waiting. The talking and movement in the small school office seemed to go on for hours; phones were ringing; a detective and two police officers were asking questions and taking notes. Through the window, Miss Dent saw the ambulance speed away from the school with whirring red lights; out into the desert, into the sun.

Mrs. Folsom was beside her then. "Are you all right, Miss Dent?" Miss Dent did not move her head or speak, she did not respond in any way; it was as though she were separate from the others and could not communicate. She only glared, took in shallow, fast breaths, waited.

"Shall I get you a glass of water, Margie?" Mrs. Folsom asked. Miss Dent nodded. "All right, then, I'll get you a glass of water. And why don't you take a seat here on the bench."

Miss Dent told Margaret's mother how sorry she was. Mr. Escoffier would not look at Miss Dent, he was too busy and distracted.

Miss Dent was driven back to the Oasis Motel by Mrs. Folsom. They did not speak. Miss Dent held her hands together on her lap; her shoulders were tense. When she got out of the car, Mrs. Folsom told her she would pick her up in the morning; her tone was commanding, but gentle. Then she handed Miss Dent a ten-dollar bill and told her to get herself a sandwich at the motel restaurant, and told her not to drink any coffee or soda tonight for she needed a good rest.

"God," Miss Dent said, her eyes closed, her palms flat against each other, "God, I know the consequence of what I have done. The consequence of what I have done is that I'll never miss anything again. I won't want anything. No desire. I'll have no wishes, God, and no discontent. Don't let me live and die here, like this, in this place, feeling this way. Make me someone"—Miss Dent sobbed—"else. Give me some new, other life, in a better place. If you *only* will take care of me now. Take care of me now."

LOVE

Along an unpaved road off the highway stood a one-story, four-room cottage, the only structure for many miles in that part of the desert. A charming path, lined with rocks and potted flowers, led to the front door. There were white curtains at all the windows, rustled now and again by a rare, small breeze. The house faced south.

One summer evening, the two women sat across from each other at the neat kitchen table. Mrs. Folsom had a mug of coffee before her, Miss Dent a bottle of warm soda. A deck of cards was between them.

"Did you wash your hands, Margie?"

There was no answer.

"Margie? I won't play cards with you if your hands aren't clean. The cards get all sticky."

"I washed them."

"Oh, and what's that tone of voice?"

"I'm sorry. I washed my hands, Mrs. Folsom."

"Well, fine. We can play our game now." Mrs. Folsom glanced at the electric kitchen clock. "Only have about a half hour, though. I want to get an early supper on tonight. You deal, Margie. Remember I taught you about how to deal?"

Miss Dent was wearing short pants and a sleeveless cotton shirt. She pulled her bare feet up onto the chair, rested her chin on one of her knees. Her tongue stuck out a bit as she placed cards on the table, seven for each of them.

Mrs. Folsom sipped her coffee and with three fingers patted the stiff curls of her hair.

"I see the moon coming up," Miss Dent said. "How can the moon come up when it's still sunny out?"

"It happens that way sometimes, Margie. This time of year, this part of the country."

"Oh, it's always too hot."

"Margie. I don't think I like that tone of voice. Not one bit." The older woman had picked up her cards and fanned them evenly, but now she put them facedown on the table. "I can't play cards with someone who sounds so mean and unpleasant and miserable all the time."

"Oh, I'm sorry, Mrs. Folsom. I won't, I'm sorry."

"I think we've talked about complaining. I think you know how I feel about complaining."

"Please, Mrs. Folsom. I don't mind the sunshine. I didn't mean to say it. Let's play our game."

Mrs. Folsom took her cards and regarded them in silence, moved one or two.

The younger woman, interpreting her own hand, gasped, giggled, then covered her mouth. The older woman pointedly ignored this display.

"What'll we have for supper?" Miss Dent wanted to know.

"Stew, I think."

"Oh, I love stew. And dark bread?"

"If we have it. And you'll make lemonade. Can you do that, Margie? I don't want a mess in this kitchen again, not like the last time—"

"I can, I can, there won't be any mess, I'll make the lemonade."

"That'll be fine then," said Mrs. Folsom, distracted, a bit weary. "Are you ready to play, Margie?"

Miss Dent nodded. She studied her cards and pulled at her bare toes. Mrs. Folsom said: "We don't play with our feet at the table, do we?"

Softly: "No. I'm sorry." She flipped a card from the stack in the center. "Oooh, oooh."

"Discard now, Margie."

Mrs. Folsom had never before seen eyes like those: gorgeous, distant eyes, eyes that changed in seconds from pale to deep, described a brilliant, mysterious spectrum of lavender, violet, lilac, with the tiniest honey-colored dots. And the hair—exactly the color of carrots—thick, full, uncommonly beautiful hair. The gorgeous eyes were narrowed now, a bit of the beautiful hair fell across the forehead, for the younger woman was concentrating on her hand. She grinned, suddenly, and pulled a card from her fan of cards, placed it on the table. "I'm gonna win, I'm gonna win," she sang softly. "I'm gonna beat you."

Mrs. Folsom shook her head sharply. "Now, Margie. Is that a nice way to play? Is that how we play?"

"No, Mrs. Folsom."

"Haven't we talked—so *many* times—all about being a good sport, playing fair?"

"Yes, Mrs. Folsom, yes. I'm sorry." The younger woman took a quick swallow of her warm soda.

The sun was changing: its bright white became hazy yellow, streaking the plain desert landscape with shadows and shapes. In this part of the country, the sun sets so quickly.

Mrs. Folsom sighed lightly, she smiled. The younger woman looked at the face across from her: all patience and generosity, ease, assurance, and safety were told in the soft breathing and smile. "And anyway," the older woman went on, drawing a card from the deck, "don't ever be too sure of yourself, Margie."

MY MONSTER

May 10

Today I passed a monster on the street. Not so much that he was frightening, except it's frightening to be so overwhelmed with pity. I was not disgusted by him, just taken by surprise.

I saw him coming toward me, towering above the lunch-hour rush of pedestrians; so it was his size I noticed first. Then, as he got closer, the details of his horrible appearance emerged, like a photograph in a bath of developer.

He was fully six foot five, perhaps even taller, wearing a brown suit and a red plaid tie. His hair was jet black and—I have no other word—bumpy, as though something was growing way up there. His body was hunched. His walk was graceless, heavy, and his arms moved stiffly at his sides. I analyzed that his shoulders were stooped from years of *attempting to seem smaller*. His features would have made any man ugly, but on him it was a crazy face, the cruelest blow; rubbery lips that frowned, a wide forehead, deep slices in his cheeks. His eyes were bright blue; the tiny pupils in his giant head showed a man tortured, criticized his whole life.

I imagined the adolescent boy-monster praying, each night, for God to please, please stop him from growing.

I had the thought that if his mind were slow, he was better off, and then hated myself for thinking it, and for staring. My temperament, my lifestyle, my sense of myself would not tolerate his oversize shoes. This monster can never sit with coffee and a paper, just watching people pass. He can never be anonymous or innocuous in the world. And what about being sexy, or cute, and flirting? What gentleness can he have known from his friends? And his family. What a nightmare . . .

June 10

I see it is a month since I wrote of seeing Robert on the street. That is my monster's name, I found out. He is a devotee of Mark Twain, practically a scholar. He is also interested in silent films. After a few days, I saw him again. I was alone on a little stone bench on the corner of Wall Street and Pine. I was having a cigarette, waiting until one o'clock when I and all the secretaries, bankers, and businessmen returned to our offices. Spring was stubborn this year, and gradually asserting itself in small waves. I was thinking of nothing, just enjoying the sun, watching the vendors. Suddenly, I was in shade. It was this giant man, standing in front of me, staring down.

I rose by instinct. His head blocked the sun out, his face was dark, it was ominous. He said something, too softly, and I stuttered: "What? What was that, excuse me?" He asked for a cigarette. I fumbled for one, as if a mugger had demanded my wallet, and meanwhile the giant arduously seated himself. He directed his face toward the sun and closed his eyes and made a low, satisfied noise.

I held the cigarette toward him cautiously. He took it with two fingers. He looked at me and his smile was truly gruesome: the teeth were a greenish color and mashed together, the gums were black. I don't know why I took my place beside him on the bench again. We looked ahead, not at each other.

He said: "What a spectacular day." I agreed. "The sun puts me in such a nice mood," said he.

This statement intrigued me. For this creature, a bad mood must be worse than bad, a nice mood can't really be much, I reckoned. And I know how superior my attitude was. I was determined to establish a distance, psychically, with ideas. In my heart, I must have felt a threat.

He talked on, casual conversation which I did not encourage. I learned he was a messenger for one of the banks, in his mid-twenties (his age was completely indiscernible), and that he was saving money to leave the city. "I'd like to farm," he told me.

When his cigarette was done, he tossed it and abruptly said goodbye. I watched him walk away clumsily, an obstacle for the crowd returning to work. Several people stared up at him as he passed, and they made remarks to each other, they seemed amused.

So I began seeing Robert every day, only for those ten minutes at the end of my lunch hour. We were acquaintances. I did not have much affection for him, actually. I was polite, but reserved. Robert's voice was very deep and he spoke slowly; he sounded like a machine talking. Our conversation was superficial, not memorable. I sensed he just needed some contact, some human warmth, fellowship.

He was always first to leave. I would watch him clunking down the street and shake my head, feeling pity, astonishment. My meetings with Robert were not wholly unpleasant, but I did not look forward to them either.

One day, a woman from my office, Rita, a loud, overly cheerful person, insisted on joining me for lunch. Seeing Robert lurk around the corner of Pine Street—he'd not yet seen me—I steered Rita into a diner, saying: "Oh, no, here comes this brute." I told Rita, very sketchily, of my association with him. She accepted the situation as I'd presented it: this Robert was a sad character and I was kind enough to tolerate him. She laughed and said: "It's so *sweet* of you to take him under your wing like that."

Robert became persistent inviting me to his apartment uptown. He said he'd cook a supper, and suggested that we could screen some silent fills; he had an extensive collection, mostly comedies. Well, I could not begin to imagine what his home would be like, and I had no intention of visiting. And I also felt the offer was inappropriate. I did not want to reject Robert, but I could not accept, so I remained noncommittal. Eventually, he maneuvered his address and phone number into my possession, and still I avoided his invitations.

I hesitate to make too much of all this. We see ourselves in others, it's true, and Robert did have this spooky effect on me which I knew was profound and which I could not grasp. But, also, after a time, he was only another person I came across during the day, an encounter that sometimes annoyed me, occasionally pleased me—a completely passionless and, yes, meaningless relationship.

Well, after two weeks of this, Robert disappeared. At first, I was relieved, thinking I had a day or so of vacation from him. But another week ended, Robert had not shown up, and I got curious. I honestly don't think it was that I missed him. But it was odd, that's all, that he should vanish.

Maybe he had found another job, somewhere else in town. Perhaps he'd taken his money and bought a farm. These were unlikely possibilities. He had not mentioned which bank he worked for, or I had forgot, and I did not know his last name. My interest to know what had become of him intensified as the days passed and he did not appear. For another week I debated whether to go to the address he'd given me. It's foolish even to consider it, I'd think. But it seemed that if *I* did not concern myself with Robert, no one would, and that idea kept me paralyzed and depressed and anxious for another couple of days. The piece of crumpled paper Robert had given me was a temptation: it meant that I could easily solve the mystery. Now—should I bother?

Robert lived in a perfectly clean, quiet, safe block in the Upper East Seventies. He was on the second floor of a five-story building. I rang the bell and was buzzed inside. On the landing stood that familiar, hulking figure of my monster, and I let out the breath I'd been holding.

He was pleased to see me, but not at all surprised. "Oh," he said, waving me up the stairs and into his apartment, "it should have occurred to me you'd wonder where I was."

Should it have occurred to him? Were Robert and I friends? I was instantly irritated. I'd seen that he was just fine, and I was ready to leave, to put the whole silly, neurotic episode out of my mind. I remember I decided to call a friend whom I'd not seen in over a year, after an embarrassing argument. We would make up and go out and just get drunk, and whisk from club to club in a taxi, laughing, being rude and wild. As Robert closed the door behind me, I realized I had been deprived for too long. I was suddenly desperate for fun.

The room was lit by a small desk lamp. The windows were closed, it was stuffy. Robert explained he had been watching some movies. He sat at a round table which was cluttered with newspapers, a few dishes and a pile of Twain's works. I sat on a comfortable couch. He told me he'd quit his job and hadn't found another. He did not seem distressed by this, which surprised me. I'd assumed Robert was terribly poor—I don't know why, unless because he held such a lowly job. "I've been very busy, though," he said. "Reading."

I could not think what to say. I was agitated. I offered him a cigarette. He asked if I'd like some wine. He took a sip from a bottle of cheap white wine and passed it to me. I was obliged to sip from that bottle, which I did timidly, uneasily. I handed back the bottle, and as he reached, his elbow knocked the Twain to the floor, volume by volume. The movement was so fast, the crash so startling. Robert rose, turned on the radio. He began arranging some papers. His back was to me.

I knelt to pick up the books. I don't know what I heard or saw, but I looked up at Robert: his huge shoulders were trembling. He turned around, facing me now, and I could see he was crying. His dirty hands, like enormous tree roots, awkwardly wiped tears from his cheeks.

He sat beside me on the floor. We did not face each other, but looked ahead, as though we were back on our Wall Street bench. He let out a tiny gasp, a child's cry, not his. And by this I was moved to comfort him. I put my hand on Robert's arm; he responded by curling his legs, laboriously positioning himself so that his head was on my lap. He held my hand gently and put his other arm around my shoulder. I can imagine that I was like some toy animal in his giant embrace; but it did not feel comical. We slept in this manner, an hour or so, I think. The room was so dark, I could not know what time it was when I awoke. I left him still sleeping.

July 10

Either I understand nothing, or there's nothing to understand.

At the end of June, I went up to Rhode Island to see my parents. When I returned to New York, I learned I needed emergency dental surgery; I spent a day in the hospital, a few more home in bed, medicated and miserable. It has been such a hot summer. Today was my first day back at the office. I took my sandwich to that same stone bench where I met Robert, and I did not think of him once.

I looked up from my newspaper to watch an argument between a fat woman and a vendor. I was startled, then, by the sound of my name being called from somewhere behind me. I turned, and I didn't recognize anyone. But I was sure of what I'd heard. Then there was a man, walking directly toward me, darting between pedestrians, waving. Who was this? School friend? Client?

I stood. My paper lunch bag blew off the bench and slapped a young woman's leg. He was in front of me, then; he extended his hand and greeted me warmly. Even this close, I could not place him. He saw that I was puzzled and embarrassed. "Robert," he said.

"Robert? Robert who?"

"Now, I know you *must* remember me."

His voice was less scratchy, less monotonous, but familiar, and so I knew. He was just my height, and slim. He wore a dark linen suit and a tie with a matching handkerchief stuck in the breast pocket. He smiled at me, wide and frank, illuminating an extraordinarily handsome, almost pretty face. The breeze caught his hair, and he smoothed it with the tips of his fingers. Bright, confident, friendly eyes. Like a movie star. I knew this was Robert, but I *knew* it wasn't.

"Well . . . oh, Robert . . . well, how have you been?"

"Not bad. New job, finally. And I even carry a briefcase." He held the object up playfully and laughed.

He was so casual with me, and I was utterly distracted. Could this be some other Robert?

I tried a test: "Given up your Twain?"

Without a pause or blink: "Oh, not at all. But, I don't have as much time now, of course."

So, I said something about my trip to Rhode Island and my dental work. And then I could not resist: "Robert, you know, you look so different. You look like a different person."

"How do you mean?" I could not decide if his bewilderment was genuine, and I still don't know.

"Is it you, Robert? Are you—?"

"Yes. It's me. I remember you very well. Of course it's me." And then something about now that he was working downtown again, we could see each other at lunch, as we used to.

"Robert, I'm so confused." This I said very softly. I was sad, and I don't know why; fearful, and I don't know why.

He leaned toward me, as though to confide or conspire. "All that matters is that we have each other. Now, I've got to run. I want to make a good impression on my new boss, you know." He stepped back and smiled. A good impression. He was so appealing, his eyes and smile and stance. Two secretaries passed; they looked at Robert, flirting, and whispered to each other, and giggled. Robert shrugged and winked at me.

I feel all alone in the world, and dazed. I sense that there is something I *need*, something I must have to actually go on living. But I don't have a clue what it is, and so I'll never find it. And so I am in this pain. . . .

"Tomorrow, at lunch," he said, and was gone.